To Cazza,

Embrace
The Weird!

EMI

EMI

CRAIG HALLAM

Published in paperback in 2020 by Sixth Element Publishing
on behalf of Craig Hallam

Sixth Element Publishing
Arthur Robinson House
13-14 The Green
Billingham TS23 1EU
Tel: 01642 360253
www.6epublishing.net

ISBN 978-1-912218-83-7

British Library Cataloguing in Publication Data. A catalogue record for this
book is available from the British Library.

Craig Hallam asserts the moral right to be identified as the author of
this work.

Printed in Great Britain.

This, my weirdest story yet, is for my favourite weird people: Tups and Craig, Stu and Steve, Amy and John, Hatts and Gillie, Tom and Nimue. Their inexhaustible support and geekiness is a salve to my odd soul.

Also by this author

Greaveburn
The Adventures of Alan Shaw
Old Haunts: The Adventures of Alan Shaw Volume II
Not Before Bed
Down Days
Oshibana Complex

Available in print and ebook.

Stay up to date with Craig Hallam

Facebook: www.facebook.com/craighallamauthor
Twitter: @craighallam84
Patreon: www.patreon.com/craighallam

Acknowledgements

*This book wouldn't exist without the support
of my amazing Patreon patrons.*

Amy – Ashleigh – Clare – Cleo – Duncan – John
Keith – Marie – Mark – Meshell – Miranda – Paul

MEETINGS

The grass had decided to become everything it could be, growing until only the barn's roof was visible above the swaying fronds. Slates had slipped, making wounds that exposed wooden ribs beneath. In the eaves, a dried bird's nest rattled in the breeze.

Christopher stood at the foot of the hill, looking up at the sagging roof. Drifting toward the dilapidated marvel, his progress could be seen as a shifting wake in the tall grass, a shark splitting water.

Skirting the barn's perimeter, he swept hair the colour of dirty butter from his eyes. Cracks and creases in the stonework grinned and grimaced. The masonry sprouted vibrant mosses and the odd weed-flower. Some stones lay on the ground, some shards of broken slate. He stood at a distance for a while, looking up and down the walls, back the way he'd come, across fields where the wind made eddies in the wild wheat that chased like swallows. He looked to the horizon simply because his eye fell there, made from a spine of hilltops, and saw beyond them to the empty prairies and meadows and clear green rivers he'd already traversed, everything silent and blooming and undisturbed.

He circled back around to the barn's doors.

They hung askew, holes gaping between mouldered

planks. The chain, so badly rusted that its links were immovable, snapped in Christopher's bare hands. Where it had lain across the door, a deep red grin scarred the wood.

The scent of ancient hay and animal dung still remained inside. Light bled through slats of the boarded window in two glistening shafts. If he still breathed, Christopher would have caught his breath.

One shaft of light came to rest on a pair of mottled legs, curled beneath a summer dress of lemon and white. It was stiff with dirt, torn and frayed at the embroidered hem. A pair of dainty white socks had yellowed with age above pretty, dust-covered shoes. The other beam caressed the crown of a bowed head, blonde locks weaving their way like a golden briar about the child's head.

Christopher tried to speak but only released a squeak of desiccated vocal chords. His unused tongue made a dry clack between receding gums.

"Ch-h-hello," he managed, in a dry rasp.

The small legs retreated into the dark. The sound of a chain dragging in dirt as the little dead girl stepped forward, uncertain in what must have been her first steps in an age. Reaching the extent of her chain, wrapped thrice around her tiny waist, the girl jerked backward and almost off balance, waving her arms to stay upright. By the light from the broken doorway Christopher could see she was seven, maybe eight years old, and had been for a long time. Her leather t-bar shoes pointed slightly toward each other at the toes. Her hands hung slack on the apron of her dress. Her right sleeve was a tatter, the thin bicep beneath shredded.

Christopher's hand strayed to his stomach, a spot on his threadbare dungarees where the rubbing had worn the denim white.

"Your name." Christopher forced the sounds from his mouth, kneeling to her.

The girl lifted her head, hair plastered across her ashen forehead in some long forgotten fever. Christopher reached out to brush it aside, a reflex he didn't realise he'd forgotten until it was remembered. Her eyes were the yellow of the Sickness. The colour of his own.

"Your name?" he asked again, his voice becoming softer with the practice, returning to its old disarming whisper.

When she opened her mouth, a moth battered its way from her lips and escaped through the wounded roof.

"Emi," crackled the girl. "My name is Emi."

Her Mummy and Daddy had put her there to keep her safe, and they were coming back. So, Emi waited. She waited until Christopher came and yanked her chain from the wall as if it were buried in sand, not stone. She waited until the world fell quiet outside, until the Sickness receded, taking most memories that she had with it. Except that Mummy and Daddy were coming back. That, she knew.

With the child free to roam as she liked, Christopher set off once more on his eternal pilgrimage without destination or purpose. The brief wonder of finding her forgotten.

Emi wandered to and fro in his wake, winding across the old track, taking in the colour of the bushes and flowers, watching insects flit and fly. Not much had survived, but the insects had.

"Where are we going?" Emi asked.

Christopher's spine snapped to attention at the sound of her voice. He spun around.

She was still there.

Christopher had to think about his answer.

"Nowhere in particular," he said.

"Oh," said Emi, regarding a wild hedgerow at the roadside. Entangled in the branches were delicate white flowers on thin vines that curled like filigree. Without a thought, she reached out to pluck one.

Christopher's hand lashed out, gripping her wrist tight.

"Don't touch that," he said with little urgency.

Still in his steel grasp, Emi asked why.

"It'll kill you."

Looking at the way his white knuckles enveloped the girl's forearm, a memory surfaced to gather air and then submerged once more, leaving only the flash of a tail. Christopher drew back his hand to stare at it. This was turning into an odd day.

"We're already dead," pressed Emi. She shifted the chain that still wrapped her waist, flecks of red drifting down to stain her dress a little more.

Christopher was admiring his hand.

"It'll kill you more."

He walked away.

Emi didn't move. Her little head tipped to the side. The flowers were so pretty, the petals so delicate.

"Christopher?"

The sound of his name on her tiny lips seemed wrong to him. At first, he didn't respond. But there was something, something he should do, an itch to scratch. He should answer.

"Yes?"

"Is everyone dead?"

Christopher stopped in the track, but didn't turn.

"Yes."

"Are Mum and Dad dead?"

"Yes."

"Oh."

A small part of him expected tears, or at least another question. He heard the sound of Emi's tiny shoes in the dirt, and felt her fragile hand slip into his own.

"We should go then," she said.

The track cut between a pair of gentle hills, blocking their view of the landscape. But as Christopher and Emi left the gulley, they found that they had been steadily climbing without noticing it. They now had an unparalleled view of the valley below in all its desiccated glory. The distant hills were darkened by an overhanging cloud, and the sky between fell in diagonal sheets.

"What is that?"

"Rain. But far away."

"I remember rain."

A crack in the earth split the valley below, surrounded by foliage turned brittle and grey. A single tree, bent with age and naked, stretched out over the crevasse. In its branches sat a figure, feet dangling as it peered down. Christopher tightened his grip on Emi's hand.

The grass crumpled to a carpet of ashen residue as they crossed it. Soon, Emi's little shoes were encrusted with it, as were Christopher's bare toes.

The figure's shape became clearer as they approached. He was naked, displaying the blotchy blue of his skin, lighter at the abdomen and flats of his hands and feet. His shoulders were wide and square, balanced atop an impossibly thin waist.

Christopher looked down at his new charge.

"Don't be afraid," he offered, because it sounded right.

"I'm not," Emi replied.

As they approached, the figure looked up from the chasm. His eyes widened at first, and then a smile slithered across his thick lips. He kicked his feet, one sandal dangling precariously from a long toe.

"Humans," he snorted with amusement. "It's been a long time since I've seen humans."

"Obviously, since you mistake us," said Christopher.

The Blue Man's eyes narrowed. "Still, you're the right shape. Once a human, always a human, that's what I say."

Christopher didn't answer.

Emi's head tipped.

"Is he…?" she asked, looking up at Christopher.

"No," said Christopher.

"Is he what?" asked the Blue Man.

"Are you like us?" she said with a child's measure of tact.

The Blue Man leaned forward on his branch, squinting at her. As his hands shifted Emi saw that his fingernails had been chewed ragged, the tips of the slender fingers gnawed rough as if in hunger.

"Not quite, my dear. Or not at all, for that matter," he said, laying a hand on his protruding ribs and bowing his head. The smile never left. "You'll find out all about it as you get older. Or not, in your case."

"Why?"

His laughter was a wet cackle. "Cute kid. Where'd you dig her up?"

"I found her in a barn."

"*Found* her? You're a lucky little girl…"

"Emi," offered Emi.

"Emi." The Blue Man's voice entered her ears like a worm, making her tallow skin crawl.

"What's down there?" she asked, motioning to the split earth.

The creature, despite himself, answered, "Home. Or the idea of it. If you're so curious, why don't you see for yourself?"

Christopher reached forward to stop her but Emi was already at the chasm's crumbling edge.

"Emi…" he began.

The ground shifted under Emi's toes as she peered into the dark where fog hung in sheets. There was a deep scent of stale air issuing from the crack, but she couldn't see anything.

"Oh, don't wrap her in cotton wool, *Christopher*. It's not as if she can die, is it?"

Christopher glared at the Blue Man who smiled and carried on. "You could always throw yourself in after her." The Blue Man scratched one serrated ear and observed the fruits on the tip of his finger.

Christopher pulled Emi away from the edge.

"Careful now, Christopher," the Blue Man said. "Children break so easily."

Christopher gave the Blue Man a look of confusion. The creature feigned shock and mimed zipping his lips.

"We're leaving now. Don't follow us," said Christopher.

"But we were just getting acquainted!" the Blue Man pouted. "Humans are so surly when they're dead."

"Goodbye," said Christopher.

Emi turned to wave, but the Blue Man's attention had already returned below.

THE LONG WALK

By day, the cloud-skimmed sun lit their meanderings; by night flocks of fireflies pestered them, lighting the way with swollen abdomens like amber marbles. This track led to another and another, without end. Days and nights rolled and rolled. They walked in silence. Eventually Emi's little shoes gave way to the abuse, throwing off sections of sole and fraying at the stitches. They had to be removed.

Emi and Christopher walked barefoot together in the dirt.

Sparse countryside gave way to a land of rolling hills and dales, decorated with dry-stone veins and the odd copse of trees. In places, short stretches of ancient tarmac appeared above the soil, long since rubbed clean of any markings.

When the road disappeared, Christopher led Emi through the grass. She stroked her ashen hands through the fronds, watching them bend and sway as she passed.

"Do you have to touch everything you see?" asked Christopher.

"Yes. Don't you?"

"No."

And then nothing more was said for a long time.

Between one field and another, the river carved through the land. It had once been named and had given its name to the town that sat where the water came around in a horseshoe. Now there were only clean waters running by a sprawling ruin. From across the water, Emi and Christopher looked at what remained of the town. The outlines of rotting rowboats stood in a forest of reeds. Once stone and mortar, the houses were reduced to crippled beetles anchored by their broken hindquarters to the earth. None had roofs, and windows had long-since become gaping holes that sprouted weeds like window boxes. A cluster of pines had rooted in living rooms and kitchens, piercing where bedrooms had once been while fighting for sunlight.

Christopher squinted along the town's old road. Something lay in the dust. A dried carcass withered on the spot. He couldn't tell if it had been animal or human.

They walked the river bank, waiting for a place to cross. If he'd been alone, Christopher would have simply walked across. He had no breath to hold, and the foot-long pike that scythed through the water caused no fear. But he wasn't alone anymore. He had Emi to think about. And even though Emi couldn't die either, there was a deep part of him that said he should search for an alternative.

Further along, where the river spread even wider, they finally spotted a bridge spanning the water like a dinosaur's skeleton. Christopher saw the height of it, the length, and the state of its crumbling slopes, but there was no other way.

Up close, the bridge had become a corkscrew where one side's huge legs had buckled. They made their way across the twisted bridge, avoiding ribs of iron that showed between plaques of wasted concrete. Christopher took the gaps in his elongated stride. Emi bounced along behind, her dress and dirty lace underskirt opening like a dandelion seed as she jumped. At the other end of the bridge was a barricade. Old cars and barrels sat welded together by mutual rust. Barbed wire petrified to brittle uselessness spanned gaps between the cars. Christopher snapped it with his hands so they could pass. Their feet crunched across ancient glass, grinding it back to the sand it had once been. But they didn't walk to the town. Christopher led them away from there in a direct route. Nothing good ever came of those old places.

THE MUSICIAN

When the rain finally came, a wind whipped it into decorative swirls. Water pooled and ran and soaked. Emi's feet gave little splashes as she walked, dappling her legs with mud. Christopher's dungarees were already so dirty that nothing could foul them more.

At first, they mistook the unusual sound as a product of the rain and the valley's echoes. It wavered like water, or burst like a single droplet hitting steel. It curled out and back again, an invisible finger beckoning to anyone who might hear it.

Rounding a bend in the track, they found a musician. She sat beneath a windswept tree, protecting her from the rain and shedding its blossom which came to rest in heaps around her, or scattered across the sprawling folds of the black material she wore, which gave no hint of a shape beneath as it rippled in the wind. A leather sash hung across her neck and shoulders holding a koto of rosewood and brass. Its strings, once white, were almost black with the blood from her fingertips. Her face could have been porcelain. A groove ran across the bridge of her nose, scalpel thin and bone deep ending in onyx beads at her temples. Only the misty white of her eyes broke its course. Her melody floated out into the valley, seeming to caress the hillsides, hugging the land as it spread.

Christopher moved past, quickening his pace for the first time. But he had to come back before long. Emi had stopped.

She stood before the Musician, listening to the weaving of the tune.

The Musician's fingers peeled back the melody as if dissecting it, opening it like a frog. The second tune with its slow, pulsing drive had an element of dirge to it that spoke of new death and grief.

"It's pretty," said Emi.

"Sometimes," replied the Musician, nodding slowly. A similar cut to that at her eyes stretched from her perfect red pout, revealed only when she spoke, a sliver of red flesh beneath the white. "And sometimes not."

Emi admired the Musician's raw fingertips, the crescents of crusted blood around her fine nails.

"Does it hurt?" asked Emi.

"Yes."

"Come on, Emi. This isn't a safe place," Christopher muttered.

"No," she replied.

The Musician smiled and her face stretched red and wide.

The music dropped, a harmony of endless rest and grateful sleep. Christopher's body screamed for him to lie down.

"Emi," he said, barely able to make the sound.

Rising in pitch, the melody became stronger, the drum of the rain taking the beat.

Tackata-tackata. Tackata-tackata.

The Musician continued to talk, but her voice was lost in the song. Her head swayed, a strand of black hair swung loose from her bun in a spider-whip. The air above her instrument wavered like a desert road.

Emi was swaying on her mud-splattered feet.

"Stop," Christopher said. "Stop playing."

Still the Musician played and played as ink leaked into his vision.

Christopher stepped forward. He had to catch himself on a lower branch of the tree when his knee buckled. A torrent of blossom fell, peppering him, and Emi, whose yellow eyes were rolling.

His stiffened flesh bunched into a fist.

"Stop it," he said, his face close to the Musician's.

Her tune shifted. Darkness receded. In tingles and pulses, Christopher's body was returned to him. He turned lazily, and caught Emi by her arms before she fell. The tune had taken her deeper then he. So deep that she slept an impossible sleep.

"Wake her," he demanded, cradling the girl in his arms.

"She will wake on her own. Consider it a gift to her," the Musician said. "Is sleep not something that humans are supposed to do? Where is it you are taking her?"

"Nowhere in particular." He plucked blossom out of Emi's matted hair.

"Are you intent on wandering forever? Until what is left of your body turns to dust as you move?"

"What else is there?"

"You have a small blessing," said the Musician. Her koto whined and thrummed along with her voice. "Despite her outward appearances."

"She'll never grow up."

"That's as may be, on the outside at least." They stood in silence for a while, just them and the music. "There is a house nearby. Take her there and let her rest."

"She's been awake for so long..." Christopher was barely listening.

"Yes. You will be welcome. And wander as you will from there."

With nothing but Emi in his eyes, Christopher nodded. She had nuzzled her gaunt little face into his shoulder, a fist near her mouth.

Walking into the rain with his dainty cargo, he left the Musician alone.

She teased a new tune. A tear, running along the groove in her face, dripped from the onyx bead.

The tune was sorrowful, repentant.

THE HOST

Daylight filtered in through the walls, nothing but paper screens on wooden frames. Vines and trees painted on the walls were silhouetted by sunlight as if Christopher were trapped between the pages of a picture book. There was little furniture except the bedroll and a chest decorated with carvings of stallions.

Emi rolled over to seek Christopher, and found him perched on the windowsill, looking out across a garden.

He was smiling at her. At least, he was trying. He'd practiced it every day since she was lulled into her unnatural sleep. He thought it might even look like a real smile by now. But a twitch in his cheek ruined the illusion, showing the strain of holding such an alien expression.

By the light of the window in that immaculate room, Christopher seemed a blasphemy. The sun fought to show something of his hair colour, once only a shade darker than Emi's own. But the dirt of ages was too ingrained to the tight fabrics of his skin and hair. Small patches at the brow and prominent cheekbones showed his true pallor but only served to make the rest of him seem more dirty. His dungarees, after untold years of storms and wear, were faded and stained, their hems decimated by contact with the road.

"You should wash," said Emi.

His smile snapped shut.

"Why?"

"You just should. It's what you do."

"Oh," he said.

Motes of pollen drifted in the sunshine as if it were syrup.

A dragonfly the size of a raven chittered at Emi from the lower branches of an ancient oak tree, mandibles fidgeting. She reached up to touch the vivid orbs of its eyes, but it darted away, lolloping through the air on brittle wings. Christopher sauntered behind Emi, all but forgotten. She was everywhere at once, touching and smelling. Beetles and worms larger than her feet scuttled for cover in her wake. A centipede thick as Emi's arm wound over her toes and away. She absorbed the garden, but there was something joyless about it. Emi was a clockwork doll, a collection of gears and springs incapable of savouring what she was compelled to explore.

When she finally turned to see where Christopher had gone, she saw the outside of the house for the first time. Only in this place, this clearing, with the garden and the insects and the sun-laden air, could that house seem possible. The second storey was smaller than the first, its roof decorated with carvings at the apex and corners. Sunlight passed through the wood and paper walls until they glowed, seeming transparent. Fungus grew from the wooden beams, some in great discs wide as balconies, or ascending in size like stairs. Others crept up the frame of the house in pale tendrils, sprouting umbrellas and cornets.

"Who lives here?" Emi asked.

"Our host."

"Can I meet him?"

Christopher checked the sun. It was starting to slip below the tree tops.

"It won't be long."

They walked together for a while, hand in hand through the garden with its numerous thickets of blossom and vine. Each time they thought they'd reached the edge, it was only another clearing in the greater garden.

Christopher looked to the tree line, a darkness etched with deep green. Through that forest, Emi slumbering in his arms, he'd come to the garden. He was certain. Three days ago. Three days of Emi's sleep. Three days of the garden and three nights of the Host, and in three days of wandering here, he'd never come back to the trees. They were always just beyond the hedgerow, just beyond the foliage.

Emi was walking away. He followed.

The dusk settled like smoke as they came back to the house.

Someone had lit paper lanterns around the house and garden. Moths big as hands jostled them, setting them rocking with their great grey wings. Some of the fungus bloomed in the dark, unfurling to soak up the moonlight. The fireflies were there again, crowding above the hedgerows, guiding Emi and Christopher home.

"He'll be awake now," said Christopher. "Try not to stare."

The main hall was bigger than it seemed. Pumpkin-shaped lanterns ran along the middle and hung from brackets at the walls. Carved birds and beasts lived in the posts that held a ceiling painted to show a single rocky peak cascading with water. Trees and flowers, trapped in wood, made cabinet doors and a table's legs, the menagerie of the garden recreated indoors.

They sat at either side of a low table, Emi with her feet tucked up under her dress, Christopher with his crane-fly legs crossed.

At the end of the hall, a pair of red curtains hung half way up the wall, making a dark archway. Emi could make out a form inside. The shape of a man lay in the wall's centre as if it were a death bed. Their host's hands were clasped across his stomach like a fossil. His suit was scarlet embroidered with leaves and trees of gold and cream. His hair was a black corona that spread out on the wall behind him, greyer the nearer his head. When his lidless eyes rolled down to regard Emi, she felt a prickling in her face as if his grey gaze were tangible.

A soft dawn light rose in the alcove.

Christopher stood, motioning for Emi to do the same. He bowed as far as his back would allow.

"Emi, this is our host."

The Host's withered lips pulled back across pale gums, displaying teeth like narrow tombstones. There was no sign of movement from his emaciated face. His voice came from the walls, or the floor, or beneath the table, a breathy scratch as if he were speaking on inhalation.

"Emi," he rasped.

Emi looked up at Christopher, then curtsied to the Host, holding her skirts like a real girl.

"Be seated." The Host laboured through his words.

An ebony pot and three small bowls adorned the tabletop. The teapot rattled, and steam began to exude from the spout. Christopher motioned to Emi to pour.

She knew this game. She had played this game before. All three cups were filled, and all three remained undrained. Just like Emi remembered, it was all pretend.

A pomegranate, sliced and broken into its seeds, lay on a painted plate. Emi picked one of the red nubs, crushing it between finger and thumb and rubbed it there, feeling the juice. Christopher watched. Placing it against the pale bow of her lips, she burst it, expecting taste and received nothing but a tacky sensation on her mouth. Disappointed, she wiped it away with the heel of her hand.

"Story," the Host rasped.

"Which story would you like?" asked Christopher. It had been the same for the last three days that Emi had slept. The first night, Christopher had insisted he knew no stories. The table had been thrown across the room, a vase exploded, the lanterns flamed and flickered until his memory was forced to return. He had told the story of the Blue Man. The second night, he had told the story of the Musician, to be safe.

"Emi," said the Host, making her name sound like pain.

"Our host wants you to choose a story," said Christopher. His eyes burnt into her, willing her to choose quickly.

"Tell me your story," said Emi. "Tell me what happened before you found me."

She'd asked this before. Christopher couldn't be sure that she wasn't asking now because they had an audience.

"It's too long for tonight," he said. "I'll tell you another."

"Alright," she said. "What is it about?"

Though the Host was silent, his eyes rolled from guest to guest.

Christopher faltered.

The air grew thick around the table. From where they sat, the Host's breathing was growing heavy. The candle flame on the table flared.

Christopher looked to Emi. The way she sat, chin propped in hands. Something from memory woke like a maggot warmed under the tongue. It squirmed for a moment and Christopher saw another room. A hurricane lamp on the floor. A girl sitting across from him, legs crossed on the blanket. She wore a vest, he remembered, laced around the hem, and her hair stuck to her face in little brown curls. Bruises on her wrists, and red strokes on her face.

A book. There was a book.

And Christopher's voice, still shaking. "There was a girl, and her name was Dorothy…"

Christopher fumbled and retraced his steps, forgetting important characters and events. His delivery was cold and without imagination. Voices. He should have put on different voices for the characters. That was how you told stories. But Emi had forgotten the story, if she had ever known it, and the Host knew nothing of Old Earth tales. So, when he was done, she clapped, and the Host's voice squeezed its way into the room.

"Good."

Christopher stood and nodded to the Host.

"And now we have to go," he said, and started walking toward the door.

He turned back when Emi didn't follow.

"I can't move," she said, with something like amusement, something like surprise.

Emi's little body quivered, setting her skirts shaking as she strained against herself.

The Host's voice came from just behind Christopher's ear even though the husk was before him and across the room.

"No."

Christopher made to pick Emi from the floor, but stopped dead a few paces away. He could feel strain on his bones, as if something had lashed themselves to his insides and was slowly tugging him apart. His arms lifted at angles to his body, legs slowly sliding aside until he stood like a gingerbread man.

Emi was moving away from him, her heels dragging along the floor before lifting free of it completely. Floating above the table, her skirts and hair shifted as if she were under water, and she drifted toward the Host.

"Emi," wheezed Christopher, as each of his ribs

seemed to repel its neighbour with the force of what was holding him.

"More," repeated the Host. His eyes were fixed on Emi.

"We don't have stories," Christopher shouted against the slow rending of his body. "We don't remember anything of the Old World. It's been too long."

A cabinet flew across the room, narrowly missing Christopher as it pulverised on the pillar beside him. The lanterns flickered. A breeze was building around the Host's alcove, blowing the curtains flat against the wall until they spread out in great velvet wings.

The Host's emaciated face was inches from Emi's nose-tip. She couldn't turn aside. A stench rose from deep in the Host, wavering in the air between them, bearing images that made Emi wince.

Great vistas of blasted earth. Winds that bore the stench of carrion. A wailing mass of limbs and chains, crushed together until they resembled the contours of a brain.

Emi tried to scream but nothing would come.

The Host's eyes shimmered, wet. Emi was so close that they nearly touched. His tongue, pale and dry, extended between his teeth until it almost touched her lips. Another exhalation of the foetid odour and Emi started to spasm, her little spine wrenched back, throwing her hair forward. Her fingers trembled as she started to gag on her tongue.

The lantern tore across the room, exploding on the curtains in a shower of sparks. The Host's eyes snapped from Emi to the flames that crawled toward him, a swarm of orange spiders, then to Christopher who was coming across the room.

The Host lashed out with his mind toward Christopher who cannoned into a wooden post hard enough to shatter it. The post's lantern bounced once and split on the table spraying flaming oil. Christopher was up again, and moving faster, throwing himself forward with preternatural strength. In one hand, what had once been a stool and was now a flaming brand was pulled back and hurled end over end toward the Host's alcove. In a blink, the curtains were a blazing arc. Sparks floated down to where the Host lay, the dry carapace of his body providing more kindling. The room filled with a guttural rasp as his scarlet suit erupted in flames.

Emi plummeted towards the ground, her body twirling in on itself.

Christopher met her in the air and landed running, his feet thundering across the carpet. He leapt through a paper wall, another, and burst out into the night surrounded by splintered wood.

He only stopped running when Emi spoke.

"You can put me down."

They were at the tree line when her feet finally touched ground. A pale froth lined her lips. She wiped it away and onto her dress.

The house erupted, crumpling inward. The faint smell of burning pine and charred mushrooms came on the air. Shuddering firelight lit the garden. Blooms began to curl in the heat, vibrant colours crisping to a uniform brown.

"I like it better this way," said Emi.

Christopher tried to ignore the seeping feeling where his stomach used to be.

"He was a bad man," he said by way of explanation. Emi didn't seem to hear.

Looking up at him, she spotted the wound across his back where the post had broken his fall. The moonlight picked out an exposed shoulder blade and two dry ridges of spine. There was no blood.

"Does it hurt?" she asked.

"No."

Like grounded stars, the last embers of the Host's home had faded until darkness prevailed in the garden. Chunks of wood popped and cracked as they cooled.

Seven figures floated across the clearing like rags hung out to dry. Their toes scraped on the ground, making thin tracks in the ash. Veils decorated with red sigils obscured their faces. They spoke to each other in shuddering whispers.

Something had been here. Something they couldn't smell or sense. Something old and sick and forgotten. Something that had to be found.

THE FOREST

Sunlight came in slivers through the canopy to light great dunes of fallen leaves heaped around the forest floor. Flakes of orange and yellow tumbled and capered through the air. The ground crunched. Christopher stood on a hidden branch, and a gunfire crack echoed out into the forest's silence. He could hear Emi behind him, or rather the sound of the leaves crunched by her feet.

Emi spotted the creature first, of course. It took several attempts to rouse Christopher from his wandering reverie.

"Who's that?"

Christopher followed her finger, feeling something that he'd forgotten the name for. Something that told him he didn't want to meet anyone else. Not after the Host and the Musician. He wanted to be left alone. But the figure Emi pointed to wasn't going to give them any trouble. Not that he could see. Still, he circled cautiously.

The statue was weather worn. Damp leaves clung to the hem of a hooded robe. Moss filled the folds, making it seem as if the material had faded in the sun from verdant green to stone grey. The face was delicately insectile, the eyes slightly too large and almond-shaped, the nose under-developed. Two dainty horns ran back from her forehead, the hair twined around and running down her back. Her face was turned up to the sun, eyes heavy with the blissful heat and lips parted.

"Who is it?" asked Emi again.

"I don't know."

"She looks sad."

"How can you tell?"

"I don't know," said Emi, already wandering away.

Christopher stepped closer to the statue, searching the immobile face for some signs of what Emi saw. There was a slight trail running down the woman's cheek, ending in a tiny droplet. Christopher had to touch it to tell that it was stone. The sculptor had carved a tear.

"You're right," he said. "She's crying."

Grey clouds had overtaken the sky, only a ripple of the sun's light peeking between. An oak tree stood head and shoulders above the rest of the forest, its lower branches empty but the topmost still held its golden crown. The branches stretched out in a wide circle, holding all other trees at arm's length.

Around the clearing, more statues formed a circle around the tree's trunk, each one the same insectile woman twisted into some stirring pose, expertly crafted from stone so that the shadows added to the illusion of movement, the stages of a dance frozen each in their time. Her hands raised or clasping at herself, the robe wide in a spin or bunched at her feet as she crouched. Whirling and begging, her head always flaccid as if the body danced against her will.

Christopher tried to see motion where there was none, but his vision wouldn't focus. Something at the corner of his eye made his head snap around. It was Emi. Weaving through the statues, following the path of the dance with her own.

Pools of night crept in under every tree as the sun finally set. The darkness was soon complete and Christopher walked with one arm out in front and Emi in his wake. That was how he came to rest his hand on another statue.

Little shards of moonlight caressed her form as the canopy shifted above, making her robe seem to ripple with breeze-tossed stars. Her arms were laden with a bundle of wild flowers; each petal intricately carved. She was casting a glance over her shoulder, the little brows between those large eyes bunched, her mouth hung open as if uttering a gasp. Christopher whipped his head around, certain that he would see something too. But there was nothing, only the vague grey lines of branches visible when they moved. And the rustle of leaves, like whispers.

Compared to the forest, the moonlight in the clearing seemed like daytime. The stone woman was on her knees this time, arms extended in front of her, hands pressed to the sides of a small wooden shrine. Emi stood a little way off, popping the heads from flowers like bottle caps and shredding fronds from ferns. Christopher studied the statue. Where the woman's hand clutched the shrine's peaked arch, a finger had broken off. Her face was hidden in the cavity between her outstretched arms. Stone flowers were strewn all around. Christopher leant in to see what hid in the shrine's shadows. A large beetle ran around the feet of a hidden figurine, a rotund man in sweeping toga, eyes closed, one hand open, the other pressed to his naked chest. A stone finger lay across his tiny palm.

Christopher picked it up. The inside was red as if the stone was coating a cluster of unrefined rubies. Then he stroked the statue, peeling off a thick layer of grime with his palm.

"She's been here for a long time," he said. When Emi didn't answer, he spoke louder. "She's very old."

Emi came out of the dark with a handful of flower heads. When Christopher looked at them, she let them fall and dusted her hands. A job well done. Her mouth bunched into a little pucker as if thinking.

"How old are you?" Emi asked as if she'd been waiting for the opportunity.

"Very old."

"Older than the statue?"

"Yes."

"Am I very old?"

Christopher tore his eyes away from the statue to the little dead girl who had become his companion.

"Yes," he said. "And no."

Emi nodded as if she understood.

The moon had arched above and was making its nightly descent, the stars slowly disappearing from the brighter horizon at their backs. But the forest floor was still painted in its night colours. With just enough light to see by, Christopher had quickened his pace. Emi was having to jog to keep up. She had asked why, but he couldn't tell her. He wasn't sure himself.

And so, they missed the final statue in the morning gloom. With her back pressed to a tree trunk, eyes tightly shut and tiny teeth gritted, her face turned away and down as if something were reaching out to her, to touch her sculpted cheek, something that filled her face with terror and loathing. It would have only made Christopher walk faster if he'd seen it.

As the sun rose and the golden forest returned, he slowed down again and by midday they came to the last trees. A stone arch stood a little way off. They walked out through this entrance marker and turned to see it. Stone flowers were carved on the posts, meeting at the arc's apex at either side of the woman's face, her features surrounded by a hood but her face perfectly emotionless, at peace. A scroll dangling beneath her chin showed words in some forgotten runescript.

Before Emi could ask, Christopher answered.

"I don't know."

There were no roads on this side of the forest, only miles of meadows with their overgrown privet borders. At a little distance, one corner of some old building wall thrust its way out of piles of rubble. Emi pointed at it, but Christopher didn't want to investigate. He didn't want to find anything else.

THE NOMAD

Christopher laid his arm across Emi's chest, stopping her dead. Up ahead, someone was walking along the track as it rounded the hill's side. Christopher watched as the stranger moved out of sight, then he let Emi go. As they reached the same turn, he looked around. Hills pressed on all sides, bedrock pushing up, making grey gashes in the land. The earth fell away to their right, dropping a long way before becoming a valley wall with glistening water at its deepest end. Rocks tumbled in the breeze. The figure was in sight again, moving along the track with the aid of a staff twice its height. Although much closer, he was still travelling away, walking slower than Christopher and Emi. They followed him for a while, keeping distance between them. The figure turned to see them once, and then continued walking. Where the track dipped low to the valley floor and there was more room, Christopher sped up, dragging Emi with him. They overtook the Nomad without speaking and hurried ahead.

"I'm tired," Emi said.

"We don't get tired."

"I am."

His eyebrows bunched. Surely the Musician's charm was done. But who was he to say how such things worked?

He checked back the way they had come. The track was clear.

"Alright."

Where a small stream ducked under the track, there was a stone bridge. Christopher sat with his back to the stones, legs folded and hands resting in his lap. Emi crossed over to the grass verge beside him, and flopped down. With her head laid on her hands, she looked to her companion.

"When I close my eyes, you won't leave me."

"Why would I do that?"

"Why not?"

"I won't leave."

Emi's eyes slid closed and Christopher was left alone.

Somewhere in the dark, a choir of crickets practised their trade. Christopher stretched out his hand and felt that the stiff lace of Emi's dress was still there. When a light rose into view along the road, he snatched his hand away and fixed his eyes to wait. The light grew larger, swinging from the tip of the Nomad's staff. The little man made slow progress, but there were no signs that Emi might wake before he arrived. Eventually, he stopped next to Christopher. Lifting the lamp out in front of him brought Emi into the light.

Taking a clay pipe from his mouth, the Nomad gestured toward Emi with it. Smoke rose from the nostrils in his forehead.

"It sleeps," he said with a voice softer than his sloping face would suggest. "A most unusual child."

"In many ways," said Christopher.

"Mind if I sit?"

"Do as you like."

The Nomad groaned as he lowered to the ground. The pack on his back almost toppled him backward as he shrugged off the straps. The lamp on his staff bobbed, setting pale blue shadows scooting around them. Slipping off his sandals, he curled all four of his toes in the grass and chuckled. Christopher found his own toes curling in the dark, but he couldn't tell what was so funny.

"I've been walking a long time," said the old nomad. Christopher could barely see his mouth, tucked away under a face that was mostly nose. "Although not as long as you, I'd gather."

Christopher didn't answer.

"Not the type for talking, eh? That's fine. I have plenty of stories to listen to. Don't look like that. They're free. That's what I do, collect stories. I think I could find one you'd like."

The Nomad rustled in his bag, scooping something into a pile on his knee. Then one by one, he lifted the crude carvings up to his lamp. Each one was different, no more than three inches high, characters made from wood of all colours.

"Don't," said Christopher.

The Nomad paused, holding up one figure. With a wide base and dainty little face, a koto across her knee, Christopher recognised the Musician when he saw her.

"You don't want to hear one?"

"No."

"Then what about telling one? You must have plenty to tell. Centuries of tales."

The Nomad brought a fresh block of wood from his bag, and a small knife from inside his jacket. With the blade poised against the wood, he waited.

"I don't," said Christopher.

"That's a shame. Such a shame. I can think of one in particular lots of my kind would like to hear." He looked to Emi, who stirred in her sleep.

"No. You tell no one about her. Do you hear me?"

"Oh, give me *something*, if only to pass the night." That little knife, poised to whittle.

Christopher sighed.

"What do you want?"

"The Sickness. Do you remember it?"

"Yes."

"Tell me."

And the Nomad began to carve as Christopher talked.

"Fast. Everything was fast. People always running. Always away. Hands and teeth. I was hungry."

"And the food ran until it ran out. Yes, I know this part."

Long strips of wood curled in the Nomad's hands, the knife rocking back and forth on the naked wood.

"No more animals, no more people," said Christopher. "And the sick turned on each other. When the Sickness passed, there was no one left. Just meat that had rotted long before it stopped moving and no one else."

"You're still here. And so is she."

"For now."

"What about after? When you were alone."

"I felt… better."

The Nomad stopped his carving for a moment to look up at his muse.

"Better?"

"After a while, the hunger was gone, and it took other things with it." Christopher stretched out his hand to Emi, but drew it back when he realised the Nomad was watching him.

The Nomad nodded, and carved.

"You know there are stories about ones like you. I have them right here. Over the sea or in the mountains," he said.

"They're lies. I've been everywhere. Walked everywhere. We're all there are."

"Every story is lies. And every story has truth." The Nomad pointed playfully with his knife, this way and that to demonstrate his point. "You thought you were the only one until you found her. What's to say there aren't more hidden away?"

They talked through the night, the Nomad probing Christopher, teasing out more of his story and pouring it into the wood. Going back and back until Christopher refused to talk any more. When the sun came up, he snuffed the lamp and they finished their talk by dawn light.

"What do you think?" The Nomad held up Christopher's carving for him to see. "A good likeness, I think."

"I wouldn't know."

"Well, trust me, it's good."

Beside Christopher, Emi lay with a thin coat of glistening dew in her hair. As she stirred, the pearlescent drops fell in a miniature rain shower.

"Good morning!" said the Nomad.

Emi looked to Christopher, who simply looked back.

"Good morning," she said. "Who are you?"

"Ah, a girl after my own heart. If your protector will allow me to walk with you, I'll tell you a story or two."

Emi looked to Christopher again. Unfolding his legs, Christopher extended toward the sky.

"So where is it you two are heading?" asked the Nomad.

"Nowhere in particular," said Emi.

Popping a pale marble into the end of his pipe, the Nomad began to draw on it. Blue smoke billowed around his head as he told his tales, taking the carving from his bag, rolling it in his palms until the old stories leaked from the wood.

"There were once six maidens," he began...

Each one fair as the other. Sisters, in fact. And they lived in a deep forest with an Oni of great power. He was huge. Bigger than a tree. His knuckles were hairy and his face like a fish with fur. It was the job of the maidens to care for the Oni. He'd caught them in a spell long ago, one they could never escape, and so they were bound to him. Each night he would go out into the woods and catch deer and fish, bringing it back to the shack that was his home. And each day he slept while the maidens rubbed herbs and oils into his rough old skin.

Now, there was a warrior at this time. Very brave. Very strong. Hearing of the maidens' curse from an old fruit-seller, the Warrior vowed to rescue them from the Oni, and take the most beautiful girl for his wife. He went to the forest's edge and tethered his horse to a tree. The forest was old and wicked and he feared his horse would break its leg in the twisted roots. So, he fought his way in on foot, cutting the branches clear with his sword. Eventually, he became lost. Walking for days and days, weaving around trees and rocks, there was no way to tell where he was. He grew hungry, his flask became empty, and still he kept walking. When his armour was too heavy for him to carry, he left it behind, taking only his sword, and still he kept walking. When dreams leaked into his waking hours and hounded him to sleep, he still kept walking. Until, exhausted and hungry and half mad, he stumbled out of the woods. There was a lake lapping at his feet, with the moon overhead brighter and larger than he'd ever seen. And in the middle of the lake, on a raft made from tree trunks and twine, sat the Oni with his fishing rod.

The Warrior knew he'd found what he was looking for. Laying the sword across his knee, he sat on the lake's shore and waited for the Oni. In time, with his raft piled high with juicy fish, the Oni used his huge feet to paddle back to the shore and found the Warrior waiting for him.

'Who are you, sat in my wood, by my lake, with a sword and stern face?' asked the Oni.

'I've come to defeat you, Oni-sama, and free the maidens from your curse,' the Warrior answered.

'You're in no state to fight me, Warrior. You're too thin and too weak. Why not eat a little first, and then we'll see what is to be done.'

The warrior graciously agreed, and they gathered wood together, building a fire on the lake's shore to cook their fish. The Oni was a good cook, and his flask was bigger than the Warrior's. They ate and drank while the moon rolled overhead, but the time soon came to talk.

'You're a gracious and civil beast, Oni-sama,' said the Warrior. 'But you haven't changed my mind. I'm here to rescue the maidens and take the prettiest for my wife. Now stand up, and we'll finish this as honourably as it began.'

'I understand, Warrior. My curse on the maidens has lasted many years. Maybe it is time.'

Standing on the shoreline, Warrior and Oni bowed to each other, and the Warrior drew his sword. The battle was long and hard. The lake boiled as the Oni roared. The ground crumbled under his feet. The Warrior's sword shone in the moonlight as it swung and stabbed and bit into the Oni's hide time and again. They were evenly matched, the Oni ferocious, the Warrior disciplined.

As the moon slipped down below the trees, the Warrior dealt a final blow to the Oni's stomach and the monster fell in the sand.

The warrior bowed to his opponent and, with great effort, lifted the huge limbs into a pose of tranquil death. The Warrior prayed for the Oni. He wanted the Gods to allow this honourable monster a place in heaven, as he deserved. He prayed until the sun began to rise and, out of the woods, came the maidens. When the Oni hadn't returned, they had started to worry and had come to find him. The Warrior stood to address them as they cried with joy, weeping and falling on each other in gratitude.

'Maidens, I have rescued you. You're free of the Oni's spell and you can come back with me. I will lead you from this place. I think I now know the way. My only request for payment will be the hand of the fairest among you.'

But the maidens were still crying.

'Fool, you fool!' they shouted. 'You killed him!'

'Of course!' The Warrior was becoming angry at their ungrateful crying.

'He was our brother! Cursed into that body and us along with him. We were his carers and he our charge. And you killed him!'

At that, the Warrior turned and found that where the Oni had lain, there was now a man. The Maidens fell upon their brother, weeping, and as they wept, they began to age, an old curse finally broken. Their beautiful faces wrinkled and shrank. Their bones showed through the skin. Their gowns hung like old sacking. And, as the Warrior watched, they fell into dust. Six maidens made sand that buried their brother on the lake shore.

Emi's eyes were wide, the yellow rings like coronas.

"Did you like it?" asked the Nomad.

"Yes. I liked when the Oni died and the maidens turned to sand," said Emi.

"I see. So, you're not sad?"

"Should I be?"

"I suppose not," said the Nomad. "I suppose not."

Christopher walked on ahead. He could hear Emi and the Nomad talking but only as mumblings beyond comprehension. He pretended that they were the babble of a river or the hush of branches, that he was alone in his wandering again. He tried to go back, to make himself the way he was before when his mind could be blank and the walking was just a thing that he did, without any drive behind it. He tried. But as his ignored companions babbled in the distance, he found himself straining his ears to hear them and once he had to fight the urge to turn and see if they were still there.

They stayed in the valley, following a track that curved around and between a series of lakes and their interlocking streams. Water seemed to be everywhere, sitting quietly for the sole purpose of showing the sun its reflection.

"And Christopher said my parents are dead."

"He's right. They are. You two are the only ones left," said the Nomad. His hands were working, the little knife a blur. Every now and then he looked up at Christopher, who still hadn't turned around.

"You told him that there were others over the sea," said Emi, looking up at the Nomad's earnest nose.

"You heard that, did you? I thought you were sleeping."

"I was sleeping. Then I woke up. I only sleep sometimes but I can lay really still."

"I'm sure you can." He stopped walking and placed a firm hand on Emi's shoulder. "I think that maybe you and him, you're all that's left."

"It doesn't matter."

"I'm glad you see it that way."

They carried on walking.

"Here, I think you'll like this." He handed the carving to her.

The little wooden girl in her hand looked familiar; someone she might have seen before, maybe the other side of glass, or in water. He'd carved the design on her dress, the wild bramble of hair, and the little eyes wide with sadness and shock.

"You got the eyes wrong."

"No, I didn't. They're just eyes from a long time ago, that's all."

The carving disappeared from Emi's hand. Christopher held it up, brandishing it toward the Nomad.

"I told you not to carve her story," he said. "I told you not to, and I told you not to let him."

"It's just a toy," said Emi.

"No, it's not. There's power in these little things."

"Let her keep it, it's her story after all," said the Nomad.

Christopher weighed the carving in his hand. Then he

threw it as far as he could manage. A small plop marked its landing in the nearest lake.

"That wasn't a very smart thing to do," said the Nomad.

"It's done."

And Christopher stalked away.

The Nomad could talk and talk and, as long as the stories kept changing, Emi would listen. "Once there were rules that kept the sun and moon going around all by themselves. A kind of magic all of its own. But not so in the new world. Things have gone back to the way they were. Ulf and Yng, brother giants who have never met, carry the sun and moon over their shoulders, climbing a great circular ladder around the world. Ulf climbs with his eyes closed, for the flame that he carries is too bright for him to do any other, which is why sometimes the sun goes dark, for he must cover it that he might rest. And forgetful Yng climbs in the dark with the stars distracting him. Because the moon is made of water, he often spills it, which is why the moon is sometimes only a sliver and sometimes bright and round as his sack empties and fills…"

Christopher walked ahead, not leaving but not waiting, not following but not leading them anywhere. The track through the valley lifted, caressing the hillside and leaving the lakes to themselves. Naked trees clustered the road, making spider web shadows on the ground.

The sky was a uniform grey that hung low and mist crept across the track from bank to bank as a pale dawn rose. By that weird light, they saw the figures.

Christopher only noticed that his companions weren't following him when the sound of their feet disappeared. Checking over his shoulder, he saw the Nomad looking around. The little creature didn't find what he was looking for and so he climbed the road's embankment. Lowering himself to the grass, he crawled to the top and peered over. Emi followed like a lemon-flavoured slug, her pale legs thrusting against the ground to move her forward. Christopher came back.

"What are you looking at?"

"Be quiet!" snapped the Nomad.

Christopher lowered himself to the ground and was soon laid in the grass beside them. His ears pricked.

The rustling of twigs and leaves came to him as if something were foraging, only constant. Dragging, then. Something dragging across the forest floor.

Where the embankment sloped downward, the trees became a thin wood. Mist curled around the roots, breaking against the moss-covered trunks. The first figure came into view, coasting through the narrow pines, followed by six brethren. They had to be seven feet tall, thin and grey as if stretched and dried in the sun. They floated across the ground, flaccid toes dragging in the bracken, one after the other. The silver coronet, from which hung their veils, glinted in the light. They were silent except for the dragging, and they didn't seem to know that they were being watched. Emi opened her mouth to ask, but the Nomad laid a hand on her in silence.

Slowly, the procession of husks was out of sight. The

trio, two dead and one not, sat quietly to make sure they weren't heard. Christopher watched the Nomad.

"Thank you," he said, eventually.

"I don't want to meet them any more than you do," said the Nomad.

"They would have left you if they had us."

"Maybe, and maybe not."

When they set off again, Christopher walked with them.

Climbing the lower slopes of a green mountain, the Nomad dropped behind. Every mile or so, Emi and Christopher stopped to wait for him and then pulled away. Christopher lifted Emi, then the little man over a stone wall. The slope rose sharper as they reached the mountain's shoulders, and boulders stood proud of the grass. Soon the rock formations towered over them as the ground levelled for a while, creating a grotto of stone and dry grass where wind played tag through the narrow crevices. The Nomad stuffed his pipe with one of the pale spheres and puffed on the vapour between catching his breath.

The sun set and they decided to wait until light to carry on. The Nomad slept, leaving Emi and Christopher watching the stars alone.

White sparks filled the sky from edge to edge, slowly turning like a nursery toy.

"There used to be stories about those," said Christopher. "They made shapes. Animals, men and monsters. And people told stories about them."

The stars reflected in Emi's wide yellow eyes.

"Tell me one," she said.

"I can't remember any."

Behind them, tucked under an outcrop, the Nomad shifted in his sleep.

Leaving his companions by the road, the Nomad walked into the forest. His canteen was empty and crossing the mountain had made him dry. Where the lakes trickled through, streams littered the woods on this side of the range. He could hear one nearby, and swerved this way and that, following the sound.

The stream ran shallow and clear over smooth rocks. Fish broke apart from each other when the Nomad dipped in his canteen. He touched it to his lips, licked them and filled it again. Above the stream's delicate trickle, he heard the rustle of leaves and turned in time to see a figure appear from the tree line, floating so that its toes dragged through the undergrowth. Another two, further along in either direction, three more on the stream's opposite bank. As he capped his canteen, they started to whisper.

Christopher looked into the woods, then along the road.

"He's been gone too long," he said.

"How long has he been gone?" asked Emi. She looked at the sky like Christopher did, at the shadows on the ground, but didn't understand.

"Too long. Wait here."

The sound of the stream drew Christopher through

the trees. At the sound of the Nomad's voice, he hid behind a decrepit tree.

One of the figures hovered in front of the Nomad, staring out over the little creature's head. Although the ghoul's veil didn't move, the Nomad answered a question and shook his head. As if moving through cement, the spectre raised a hand, to show what it held. Christopher couldn't see. The Nomad's face paled visibly. He nodded. Spoke. Pointed along the stream. In unison, the priests turned and floated away.

Christopher grabbed the Nomad as he walked past, hoisting him until all four of his toes dangled above the earth.

"What did you tell them?" he snapped.

"Christopher, you frightened me. Put me down."

"No."

"They know about her. They want her. Do you know how rare she is? And you, for that matter. They want her and they're looking."

"You sent them away."

"For now, but they can find me any time they want. They can hear me, smell me, but not you. Unless you're right in front of them, you'll be safe."

"I want you to leave."

Looking up into Christopher's amber gaze, the Nomad gulped.

They found Emi sat on the grass. A pigeon had landed on her, mistaking her for a rock or a branch. She sat with it in her lap now, plucking the feathers from its stiff wings until they lay in a matt in front of her. She held up the partially plucked carcass.

"I found a bird."

Christopher's shoulders heaved. Closing his eyes, he pinched the bridge of his nose. He remembered that helping once. It didn't now.

The Nomad patted Emi on the head.

"Bless you, you're not all there, are you?"

"All where?" asked Emi.

"Never mind. I have to leave, Emi. It's best. It's safer." He looked to the gangly bodyguard beside him, a face like stone. "For me as well as you."

Her little fingers dug into the bird's side again, yanking on a feather. She blew on it, watching it float for a while and come to rest with the others.

"Okay."

Shouldering his pack and taking up his staff, the Nomad patted Emi's head before walking back the way they'd come.

THE CITY

Snow blew in from the mountains, blanketing the earth with rolling sheets so white they were blue. Emi and Christopher left the roads and struck out across the tundra. Everywhere was heavy with the snowfall. Trees groaned under the weight, the sky hung low in a solid grey sheet. Chevrons of birds cut across the clouds on their way to somewhere warmer. Emi's arms pumped, her shoulders providing the force to drag her through the waist-deep snow. Each day the snow melted a little and refroze, making a crispy topping that Christopher's bare feet had to punch through. They were always wet, but never cold. When the snow storms came, Emi walked behind Christopher with her hand gripping the back pocket of his dungarees. The sun rode the horizon, barely lighting the sky or warming enough to melt the snow, seeming to direct its rays straight into Christopher's unblinking face.

Weeks of walking passed before Emi slept again, laying on the ground and growing still as the winter around her while Christopher watched.

The snow continued to fall. Christopher marked the spot where Emi lay with a fallen branch and waited, the snow building around him as he stared out across an untamed world.

Only once did he nearly lose her, returning from the void of his reverie to find the branch gone, perhaps fallen in the wind or from the weight of the snow. He dug for four days in the snow drifts until he found her again, unmoved, still sleeping. When she woke, her tiny hand punching through the snow in a huff of white, he pulled her up like a weed.

Eventually the snow became rain. Freezing slush squirted between their toes. The sun picked up momentum, hurtling higher and higher with each sweep of the sky. The cawing of bird armies was deafening as masses of wings blotted out the sun, and with the first warm showers, banks of yellow trumpets erupted from the ground. Over the fields below, a swarm of swallows made liquid movements in the air.

When they found the first building, Christopher wondered whether to turn back. Four storeys high, one side of the building was torn away as if a giant caterpillar had taken a bite. Emi climbed over the crumbling masonry to get a better look at the nothing that had been left behind. Christopher hung back. In his mind's eye, the horizon pulsed as if the sun had crashed to earth. A rolling plume of heat and smoke that knocked him rolling for miles, coming only to stop when something broke his momentum. In the present, his throat felt tight. He called out to Emi for her to return, insisting that they go around, but this time Emi wouldn't have it and he was forced to follow.

As they walked through the ruins, rubble became

a constant carpet underfoot so they had to weave and stumble to make any progress. More buildings sprouted from the ground, some only sections of wall in the debris. Trees torn from the earth lay dead, some leaning with a few roots still buried, others pulverised to bracken. Still, inward they went. They finally reached an area where even bricks and mortar had been reduced to a thick dust, a circle of scorched earth where nothing would ever grow again. Dusty glass crunched underfoot. The few structures left standing were only cardboard cut outs among chunks of masonry. Emi walked over to a wall where a silhouette was burnt onto the surface, a figure with another crouched beside, a gruesome shadow theatre. She touched it.

"Come away from there," said Christopher.

Emi was looking around at the devastation, one side of her mouth curled in a smile.

"What happened here?" asked Emi.

"Desperation," he said.

Christopher stood while Emi explored, barely bothering to watch her. What had the Nomad said? She wasn't all there. Christopher remembered little girls. The smells and the laughs and every look their eyes could make, how they squealed when they played in the park. He remembered hearing a playground before he saw it. The flap of little shoes, the *skitch-skitch* of a skipping rope and the high-pitched chanting of little witches. Watching Emi pick through the wreckage of a city, fascinated by the charcoal shapes of long-dead people, the remnants of everything human there had ever been, Christopher started to wonder what he'd found in that barn, because it wasn't a little girl.

The sound of shifting rubble made him spin around.

Emi was gone.

Searching the rubble for a foot, a hand, a strip of lemon dress, he darted up the mound. Where the earth had become a hole, Emi lay a little way below at the centre of a shaft of light, next to an ancient lorry. The cab was on its side, glass intact but thick with dirt. The trailer stretched up the sinkhole's other side until it was almost vertical. Rust had destroyed most of the trailer until it lay open like a seashell. Christopher slid down into the hole, finding Emi sitting against the cab. She held out her arms to be lifted. Christopher scooped her up and began to knock dust from her dress.

"I fell," she said.

"You're not damaged."

The cab thumped.

They froze.

Christopher put his hand over Emi's mouth as she tried to say something.

The cab thumped again. Flakes of rust floated down around the old vehicle. Setting Emi on her feet, Christopher crept over to the cab and tried to peer through the window. Nothing. Just dirt and darkness inside.

Thump.

Christopher jerked back. Emi was at his side, a brick in her hand. Before he could stop her, she had smashed the window and was peering inside.

"Who's there?"

She soon retreated when the lorry's inhabitant slithered out of the dark.

Held up on two hands, it dragged a ruined body behind, one leg and a grey coil of tattered guts. As it came into the sun, its single undamaged eye roved in the light. Heaving itself over the rubble toward them, it didn't speak. Where there had been a jaw was only a sliver of tongue hanging from the open neck.

Emi backed away to clutch Christopher's leg.

What had once been the lorry's driver crept toward them, displacing rubble with a wet scraping sound. When it drew near, it stopped, its neck craning up to Christopher's face, the head tilted and the single eye searching him. Lying on its shredded stomach, the driver reached out a hand, softly stroked the hem of Christopher's trousers, twitching back when the denim proved real. The eye swung in its socket, lubricated by a faint glimmer of liquid. Then the driver turned to Emi, and reached out again. Her lip curled as the frayed fingers touched the lace of her dress. In its throat, the driver made a soft keening that could have been words if its luck had been better. The brow over its glistening eye bunched, lifted.

Emi's little foot slammed into the pathetic creature's temple. Again. And again. The driver's eye swung toward Christopher's slack jaw and wide eyes. Then it popped as Emi's heel punched through, crushing the front of the soft old skull and tearing away what was left of the driver's face. Christopher's backhand knocked Emi from her feet and clear into the air. He dove to the driver, tried lifting its head, but what was left fell apart in his hands.

Emi lay across the bomb hole where she had landed, spread-eagled in the dirt and still. She didn't bother to get up when Christopher stalked over. Grabbing her by both biceps, he lifted her to eye level.

"Why did you do that?" His teeth snapped in her face.

"It was a bad thing," she said.

"It wanted help."

"Like the Host?"

Christopher cooled.

"That was different."

"How?"

Christopher could feel Emi's thin bones bending as his grip tightened. He could break her. Break her and have done with it.

"Christopher, you're hurting me."

His hands snapped open before he could think. Emi picked herself up and began to dust her dress. Christopher was shaking his head.

"I can't hurt you," he said. "I mean, you can't be hurt."

"But you were going to. I could tell." She looked down at her feet where the creature's blood had formed tiny red shoes. "Look. Just like Dorothy."

Christopher stalked away, hands pressed to his temples in an old gesture newly remembered. Clambering up the bomb hole's side, he was gone. Emi stood for a while, taking in the hole, the sunshine, and the sad stain left by the creature. Then she followed.

THE CARAVAN

Christopher had stopped taking notice of the land around him. The sound of earth under his feet was only on the edge of hearing. Walking in silence, his eyes became unfocused on the road ahead. He wandered for centuries like this, as if following something that stayed just out of sight. His mind blank. The memories buried deep. It wasn't the same now. Only a thin layer of dirt separated fractured images from recollection. His striding meditation was constantly interrupted by images and sounds. He kept thinking of little fingers with tiny fingernails. Dresses and picture books. Cellar ceilings that rained dust. Or hunger. A crunching wetness. Gnashing and screaming and pleading. Bright flashes, fire, winds that carried him like tumbleweed. And waking, after it all, to an empty world. With his attention so inwardly fixed, Christopher was oblivious to the world, a kind of moving hibernation that even Emi struggled to break through.

An old wooden caravan was what finally caught his attention. Decorated with carved fascias painted bright colours and with large wheels which shook on their axles, at one end the caravan was pushed by a beast that towered over him, over the caravan's curved roof, an embroidered green drape over its back, something of an ox and something of an earless elephant in its ancestry.

Each of the beast's steps seemed to come from a place of deep weariness. Its neck and shoulders were braced against the caravan's end wall so that it constantly faced the ground. At the other end of the caravan was a porch and, standing at the rail, a figure. Its face was one large brow. Scratching at the apron of fat that hung low over its knees, sucking its tiny teeth, it regarded Christopher.

"Ho there, I said." Jowls shuddered and continued to move even after the speaking was done. The voice was feminine, but muffled by great mounds of flesh. Raising her brow, the Gypsy's eyes appeared as if from under a breast like smuggled gems.

"Yes?" offered Christopher.

"You dead?"

"Yes."

"Blow me!" The balustrade creaked under the Gypsy's weight. "Come here. Let me look at you."

"No."

"No need to be like that. Just curious is all."

"You're always curious. All of you. Curious enough to take us apart and see what's inside." Christopher started to walk away.

"Us? There's more of you?"

He knew he'd said too much and waited too long. Emi wouldn't be far behind. She might have slept once, maybe twice in the past few weeks but his lead never lasted. Sometimes she wandered, swinging her feet in wide arcs with hands stretched wide, but sometimes she ran and ran as if enjoying the feeling, making up the distance. She was never close enough to see, but always close enough that he could feel her. He had to go before she caught him up again.

"No," he said.

The Gypsy eyed him, a bottom lip like raw liver pouting up under her nose.

"Not sure I believe you, son."

"We're not related." He could already hear Emi. Getting close. Sometime since the ruined city, she had remembered how to skip. Her feet made an unnerving *skitch-skitch-skitch* in the dirt. He didn't look in case she was there. "I have to go."

"Got somewhere to be?"

"No."

"Then what's the rush? Oh, I see."

Leaning dangerously over the rail so that it cut into her stomachs, the Gypsy spotted Emi. She was still a distance away, but drawing closer.

"Nowhere to go but somewhere not to be, eh? Leaving a little girl behind, son. That's not very nice."

"She's not a little girl."

Drawing closer, Emi stopped to look at the enormous beast, the caravan, the Gypsy, and then her former companion.

"Hello, Christopher." No answer. Then, to the Gypsy, "He's grumpy."

"I can see that," agreed the female creature. "Why'd this horrible man leave you behind?"

"I was naughty, I think."

"Oh, what could you have done that was so bad? I don't believe it for a second. Now, look at your little feet, they're black bright! I insist you come up here and ride with me for a while." Emi didn't hesitate in climbing the porch steps that hung over the road. "Poor thing. Poor, poor thing. And what of you, son? Not that I think you deserve a ride."

Emi's hands grasped the balustrade's spindle-like bars with the Gypsy towering over her; she could have fit inside the creature twenty times over. She stared at the space somewhere behind Christopher's head. Those eyes. Yellow, just like his.

Christopher thought of walking on. He was done and this was best. In time, he could forget. Retire to the road again. The safe and thoughtless void.

His foot found the bottom step, and he climbed aboard.

Oddments in metal and clay and wicker hung or stood everywhere. Christopher sat on the caravan's floor with his crane-fly legs crossed. The Gypsy nestled Emi in her immense lap, the little girl curled in folds of bright-coloured skirt like a hammock. One thick hand stroked her hair. She seemed to be asleep. Christopher knew that trick. He sat, eyes trained on her as if sharing a cage with a slumbering tiger that could wake hungry at any moment.

"You two been walking a long time. I can tell. I know the look of a traveller when I see it. I got the same look," the Gypsy said.

Christopher took in the creature from east to west. A mountainous creature.

"You look nothing like me," he said.

"Maybe not on the outside."

"Not on the inside either. Where are you going?"

"Everywhere and nowhere, son." She reached down to a large green hookah by her chair with its wide and ornate pewter base. Taking the metal stem into her mouth, the Gypsy sucked. Blue vapour escaped from her upturned nose, rising to join a cloud that escaped through the roof. She offered it to Christopher. He shook his head.

"Not to a city. Not anywhere with others like you," he said.

"He thinks the danglers are coming to get us," mumbled Emi. It was the first time she'd spoken since they climbed aboard. "He thinks they're going to take us away."

"Danglers, you say? Skinny fellas, float around like strips o' rag?"

"Mhmm." The girl nodded, slowly.

Christopher shot Emi a look, but she closed her eyes.

"Collectors is what they are. Although Danglers I like just as well. They give me the willies. Anyways, I got everything I need right here. No need to be anywhere, or with anyone else. What about you?"

"I don't need anything at all." Christopher nodded toward Emi. "Neither of us do."

"Now, that ain't true. This little one needs something. She needs a way. She needs you to show it to her. Though you don't know it, you need her a little too."

Christopher humphed. Emi was spying on him through half open eyes then closed them again.

"If your manners are anything to go by, you do. Food and warmth and shelter ain't all there is. Lucky for you, there's more to life. I use the word loose, you un'erstand."

"No. I don't."

"Maybe what you need is to try a little harder."

Emi stirred in the Gypsy's lap.

"She sleeps just like a log."

Christopher couldn't argue with that. It was easy to mistake Emi for wood. A little puppet with no master that followed him around, strings trailing in the dirt.

"Why don't you try some of this?" The Gypsy handed the hookah stem to him. "Might even help you relax."

Christopher took it, but only sniffed the tip.

"Ain't going to kill you, now is it?"

That was true, but he handed it back anyway.

"Fair enough, son. Not sure it'd do nothing for your kind, anyways."

The Gypsy watched Emi as the girl stood by the beast, stroking its shin, which was all she could reach. The creature didn't seem to notice. Its eyes, like oysters set in stone, were fixed on the ground. It nuzzled some grass, then took a bite out of the road leaving a pothole. Somewhere in the massive jaw, gravel crunched.

"Does it have a name?" she asked.

"Not like yours," said the Gypsy. Sat by the caravan's door, she stirred a bowl of fluid with a thick finger.

Something flickered there, an image perhaps, and was gone. "It's a Gaum. They don't have names, nor much brains. They know how to push and pull and that's about it."

Emi tested the name out a few times. "Gaum. Gaumgaumgaum."

The caravan opened. Christopher came out like a ghost train skeleton, eyes roving.

"You sleep well?" asked the Gypsy.

"I don't sleep," he said.

"Looked that way to me. Only your eyes was open."

"I don't sleep. I was thinking."

"Thinking's good," said the Gypsy, nodding.

He pointed to the bowl in her lap where light rolled as if through a submarine porthole. He walked over for a better look. "What's that?"

The Gypsy tossed the deep red contents over the balustrade.

"Just checking the weather," she said. "Rain'll be coming soon."

He looked up at the sky, blue from edge to edge.

"Soon," she said.

"Why have we stopped? I thought you travelled. Always moving. Everywhere and nowhere."

"Just resting the Gaum. Some things still need to eat, you know. Don't worry yourself. You're safe with me, son."

Emi walked under the Gaum as if it were a bridge, curling round and round the trunk-like legs, one hand trailing. Where the tassels of its covering hung low enough, she teased them like a cat with string.

"She's unique," said the Gypsy. "Never been nothing like her before and never will again."

"Take her, if you like her."

"You mean that?" The Gypsy's head spun around, jowls flapping.

"You like her. You keep her," said Christopher.

Emi was patting the Gaum, talking to it. It regarded the earth beneath it all the same.

"But she'll get bored of it soon enough," he said, sitting down on the porch steps so his large feet dangled. "At least the beast is too big for her to kill. I don't know about you."

The folds of the Gypsy's face fell and lifted by degrees. "Whyever would she do that?"

"I don't think she knows. She's broken," he said.

The Gypsy eyed the child, and shook her head.

"No, no. She ain't yours to give away." She waved a hand and the baubles on her wrist jangled. "And you should be careful how quick you are to leave her behind. What were you before her? Eh? Just a-wandering with no mind and no purpose. That ain't no life. No... unlife. Whatever you call it. She stops you just existing, son. Defines you. Look how she plays. She's a little marvel."

The Gaum snorted through the nostrils in its neck, blowing Emi's hair horizontal and almost knocking her over. The girl giggled. The sound made Christopher's teeth try to crawl to the back of his mouth.

Fields packed with yellow flowers filled the twilight with the heavy scent of pollen. Overhead, someone began to switch on the stars. The caravan wobbled past hedgerows filled with white flowers, pitching left and right dependent on the road. The Gaum's footsteps and a chorus of crickets were the only sounds. The Gypsy and Emi sat on an old swing bench on the porch. Christopher stood at the banister.

"You don't look comfortable over there," said the Gypsy. "Why not come sit down?"

He didn't reply, but scanned the road behind, and then over the hedges at either side. He'd been doing it for an hour or more.

"What're you looking for?" asked the Gypsy.

"I thought I heard something. On the road."

The Gypsy got up, making the bench swing so Emi had to hold on. She took Christopher's arm and led him across the porch.

"I never heard nothing. There's nothing to hear. Come sit down. You might not need to, but you're making me nervous."

Christopher took another look, then let himself be led.

"You're too jumpy, Christopher," she said.

"It keeps me safe."

"You've had some bad times, I can tell. Prob'ly met a few of my kind that're less than friendly. I met plenty myself. But we ain't all the same. Take a look at you two. I heard dead humans were nasty things. Savage. That's what they say. No mind of their own. Can't even talk. They just moan and shuffle and eat each other. But that ain't true, is it? Well, apart from the moaning." She elbowed Emi who chuckled on cue. "Now how about someone tell a story to pass the time?"

"Your kind like stories," Emi said.

"There's power in a story, little one. Same goes for names. Before the Old Earth you had your beginnings in, there was another afore that, where folks like me used to walk. One that ran on stories and naming things as they were made new. Humans were few, and huddled around their fires, telling stories to teach lessons to each other, to keep things away, and every tale they told of us gave us power. Those of us whose stories were told enough were gods. Others of us just monsters. And when the humans got smart enough, they stopped telling stories and started *explainin'* things. The power was gone when the stories was gone, and so we went home."

"I've seen it. The Blue Man showed me. But it was just a hole with darkness inside."

The Gypsy shook her massive head.

"We all have different ways of passing from our home to yours. Some find it at the bottom of a lake, or in the sound of crying. Some in the moonshadow of an oak tree." She snorted. "Humans weren't so smart. They didn't last long, as these things are measured. And when they was gone, we came back. Now things is as they should be again, with my kind left to roam free and humans all gone. Closest thing left is you two." She booped Emi on the nose. "Course, with no people walking around telling stories and believin', there ain't no power neither. So, we amuse ourselves in all kinda ways." The folds of the Gypsy's face spread into what could have been a grin as her bulbous finger pointed ahead. "Like the lady just over that hill, for instance."

Christopher had been barely listening until that point. He knew that old tale already. But now he turned, looking ahead, and saw the raincloud as it floated their way.

Thunder black and only a few feet across, a constant torrent spilled out of the little cloud. A figure rode beneath it, the cloud stationary above her head so that her blue scales shimmered with the constant downpour of her personal thunderstorm. She sat statuesque atop a hump-backed boar which huffed between its tusks as it carried not only the female creature but the large leather packs slung across its back, and towed two cages on rattling wheels. The rider had a bow slung across her shoulders, a quiver on the saddle by her right boot. Also, waving as the boar shifted its weight, a long spear quivered in the air, all-but tickling the cloud's underside.

The Gypsy continued, "She likes to hunt things."

Christopher darted to his feet.

"Emi, we have to go."

"Sit down, son," said the Gypsy, pouring power into the words. Christopher's bottom hit the floor. "There ain't nowhere for you to go except with her, now."

The Gypsy approached the railing of her caravan and waved a tree trunk hand at the approaching creature.

"Ho, Huntress! See that your job is done for the day!"

Christopher turned to Emi with difficulty, the Gypsy's words fixing him to the spot. The yellow rings of his eyes burned fierce as he spoke with urgency.

"You may not understand this world or how it works, how it came to be or what the purpose of it is, but know this, Emi, this thing and the thing that approaches, they mean you harm. You have to run away."

Emi looked at him with her head cocked. Her brow furrowed. Christopher had never used so many words in all the time she'd known him. She regarded the Gypsy's turned back and the approaching Huntress beneath her rain cloud. The moment strung out, uncertain, until she slid from the swing seat, her bare feet making no sound on the porch's boards. She looked between the Gypsy's mountainous back and Christopher.

"And what about you?" she asked.

"Do you care?" Christopher asked, watching the approaching Huntress from the corner of his eye.

"What does caring feel like?"

"Like… you don't want something to go away."

With that, the thing that once had been a girl put her hand into Christopher's and he felt suddenly free. He could stand, and so he did. Scooping Emi under his arm, he thought about leaving, but had one last thing to do. With a slam of his heel, he kicked the Gypsy head-first off the front of her caravan. She screeched, the ground shook with her collision and, as the Gaum paid no mind to the blockage ahead, the caravan rolled right over her. The last sound was the wet crunch of flesh and bone as the Gaum's feet were splashed with gore.

Christopher saw the Huntress then, much closer, draw her mount to a stop as she watched them. Vaulting the side railing, he darted into the forest. With preternatural speed, the Huntress leapt from her mount and plunged after them.

THE HUNTRESS

Low-hung branches seemed to lance out of the forest's half-light, scratching and tearing at Christopher and his clothes. The floor was a net of tricking vines and roots that sent him stumbling, but always keeping his feet and his momentum. With Emi still tucked under his arm, he barrelled on regardless.

The first arrow slammed into a tree just as he passed it. The wood splintered, dappling him with bark and moss. The second hit him square between the shoulder blades like the slap of a hand, which only made him stumble for a moment before finding his stride once more.

The sound of whipping air.

Christopher hit the ground.

Getting to her feet, Emi dusted off her dress and looked down at him.

"Run. Hide," he said.

Turning on her heels, Emi did as she was told, scampering off into the forest with what was more of a swift skip than a run. But there was nothing he could do about that. His legs were caught in some thick twine with small rocks tied in pairs to either end. A device for snaring. The name wouldn't come to him. As he set to prying at the ropes, the Huntress approached in a blur, not losing one step when she slammed a flying knee into his chin as she hurtled by. Christopher's back slammed into the ground with the sheer force of the strike, but there was no pain and it was nothing for him to sit right back up and continue his task.

Up ahead, Emi wove through the foliage with little urgency. Spotting a long yellow worm in the undergrowth she stopped for a minute, watched it, and crushed it beneath her foot before skipping off again.

The sound of whipping air, and her face hit the ground, golden hair splaying around her. She didn't even try to move.

The Huntress approached, serpentine and powerful in her movements, circling her quarry, an arrow nocked and ready. Her scaly blue musculature peeked out between the wild furs and leathers of her clothing, the rain that followed her making her exposed skin shimmer like a fish. But the girl might as well have been a fallen tree for all she moved. Throwing her head back, the Huntress let out an ululating call at the top of her lungs that shook the canopy above, her personal raincloud pouring a torrent onto her upturned face.

Overgrown and gnarled with vines, the clearing was a poor one in Christopher's opinion. Stretching one leg through the bars of his cage, his toes almost reached the ground between the Huntress' cart's wheels. A cracking sound made his leg jerk as the Huntress stalked past and smacked his foot with the end of her spear. There was no pain, but Christopher withdrew his foot anyway.

Towering over Christopher, the Huntress moved statuesque and fluid, in a way he remembered some animals did. Her noseless face was elegant, her eyes a corona of fierce red piercing from the smaller blue scales around them.

Emi sat quietly in her own cage, which had horizontal bars bisecting the vertical to stop her smaller form from escaping. She was humming. There was no tune to it. Even bees chose a note and stuck with it, but not Emi. Her humming grated on the senses, defying the mind's desire to find form in it.

The bars of her cage shook as the Huntress slammed her hands against them.

"Silence, little thing!" she spat.

Emi stopped for a second, regarding the Huntress' scaly countenance, and then carried on humming. Christopher's face twitched, something at his mouth, an odd sensation that he couldn't place.

The Huntress snarled, spinning away and retreating to a distance where the sound would at least be lessened. Hunkering down against a tree, she laid her spear across her lap and waited in the rain.

"Let us go," Christopher offered.

The Huntress gave a mirthful snort.

"We are no good to you. You can't eat us."

"Eat?" The Huntress gave a rattling laugh. "No one in their right mind would want to eat you. Rotten meat and thoughts."

The sun set cold and unseen beyond the canopy, towing

a silver moon into its place. The floor of the forest shifted with the dancing of the branches above. The forest was silent. Christopher saw them first, spectres gathering in the darkness, floating as if on invisible hooks, their toes dragging, breathless faces hidden by thin veils painted with a red sigil.

The Collectors wafted into the clearing, gathering unevenly around the Huntress and her captives. Some weren't even facing them, but stared off, if they had eyes at all. Christopher had the feeling that sight as he knew it wasn't at use here.

The Huntress stood to greet them, but was ignored entirely.

One Collector, indistinguishable from any other, hushed past Christopher's cage to stop before Emi's. From where its lank hands sat crossed before its body, it opened one to her, showing the small wooden carving in its palm.

Emi took it, holding it up. It was her. The Nomad's carving, with her story inside.

Christopher's stomach lurched.

The Collector extended one hooked finger through the bars, towards the thing that was once a girl. With one hand clutching her effigy, Emi reached out and wrapped her tiny fingers around the twig-like appendage. There was a moment of stillness. The Collector seemed unmoved, or possibly thinking.

Emi's hand snapped to the side.

The Collector threw back its head with a piercing

screech, the folds of its veil falling into a wide, shrieking mouth. Its brothers joined in the cataclysmic scream, until Christopher thought the moon might shatter. It reeled back, its finger bent backward at every knuckle.

Christopher's head started to ring. The Huntress was clutching her hands to her head, bent double. She looked like she might be screaming, too, but he couldn't hear it. Emi swayed back on her heels, a neat little smile stretching her face.

Breaking apart like a shoal of fish, the Collectors' ephemeral forms disappeared into the darkness of the forest, the screech dissipating to whispers. All but one. It hung by the Huntress who, now that the screeching had subsided, seemed to be listening. She bowed her head as the last Collector wafted away.

With fresh purpose, the blue-scaled creature gathered her things and headed out into the night without a word, leaving them alone in their cages.

Christopher rattled the bars. The cage rocked on its wheels but there was no give. Not even to the strength of the Sickness. As he looked over, Emi was trying to fit between the bars of her own cage. She pushed and pushed until one of her shoulders popped from its socket and a rib cracked with a loud *clunk*, but it did her no good. The Huntress had planned too well. Moving back into her cage, Emi popped her pieces back together easy as lacing a shoe.

Without the Huntress' certain footfalls, the dragging glide of the Collectors, or Emi's humming, the night fell silent but for the rustle of things in the undergrowth, and the creak of growing trees. Sitting in their cages, Christopher and Emi were silent as well. There was nothing for it. They were trapped. Christopher had examined the dense wood housing the metal bars. It might take fifty or a hundred years to rot so that he could break them free. They would just have to wait. And so he sat back, eyes growing glassy as he stared into the undergrowth.

Emi watched him, and then sat back herself. This was just like being in the barn, but better. She could see. There would be weather and maybe birds. There would be sunlight. She regarded the thrice-wrapped chain which still decorated her waist, and then Christopher. At least she wasn't alone. Stretching out, she summoned the sleep from the corner of her mind where the Musician had hidden it, and fell into a slumber.

Christopher's eyes danced into focus as the cage's wheels hit a stone in the road. He searched around. They were back on the road they had left, as far as he could tell. His cage swayed, the wheels squeaking at odd intervals as the Huntress' boar towed them along the track. She sat atop the beast once more, her back swaying with the motion of its powerful shoulders. Emi stood at the bars of her own cage, bathing in the moonlight that cast criss-cross shadows on her form. So, the Huntress hadn't abandoned them, but only gone to fetch her creature. He wasn't sure if he felt relief or disappointment.

As the night moved toward moonset and the opposite

horizon began to show licks of colour, they rode on, uncertain of their destination. By the time the sun had painted psychedelic slashes in the clouds, they came to a round in the bend. Passing by without a pause, the Huntress didn't seem to register the toppled hulk of the Gypsy's caravan where it had run off the road. It lay in the field, axles broken, its curved roof lopsided and melancholy and, in the distance, at the furthest edge of a vast meadow and still moving arrow straight and painfully slow, was the Gaum, who seemed not to have noticed that either his driver or his burden was gone.

"Where do you think he's going?" Emi asked.

"I'm not sure. Maybe he'll just keep going."

Approaching an old dirt crossroads, the Huntress turned them down another track. There had been a signpost at one corner, but the post was broken and the words on the lop-sided board had long since worn away.

Days and nights passed in nature's no-man's-land. The Huntress slept in the saddle, only stopping to shoot birds with her bow and then return to her seat to crunch them, feathers and all.

But soon a city shifted into view, off to the left of their little wagon train. A new city, raised after the fall of mankind by those who had been before, and had come again.

HOME

Helixes of smoky glass rose out of the meadow, twenty storeys tall, coming to glistening tips, far overhead. At their centre, a single column of brass stood head and shoulders above them all, the sun heliographing from its curved sides, the beams splitting into rainbows as they hit the glass towers. Christopher shuddered, marvelling at the sensation. He had forgotten what a shiver felt like. He hadn't been cold or afraid since before the Sickness took him, but now, as the Huntress rode them into this peculiar city, a part of him whispered, *You shouldn't be here.*

He couldn't help but notice the similarities to human cities, like the creatures had purposefully built this warped facsimile. Or, perhaps, humans had seen cities like these when the race was still young, and the desire to mimic had lain dormant in their imaginations for millennia. Where they passed the feet of the spires, which seemed to have been grown rather than built, shapes could be seen moving inside, back and forth, sometimes tall and thin, sometimes short and squat, depending on the distortion of the glass walls.

Further in, the city became a veritable zoo of activity. Wagons and canvas-topped stalls began to appear as they traversed a heaving marketplace. They could recognise definite streets and roads leading between the immense spires, and through it all, creatures of every size, shape and shade walked the city streets. Some darted, capered or scuttled, others lumbered or sauntered, propelling themselves on every combination of limbs and appendages. Clothes of stunning embroidery mixed with nakedness. Above, shapes hovered and swooped. They passed the foot of a building where the glass had grown like an ancient tree, with holes between its roots making caves for the creatures, inside which, illuminated by a soft glow from the walls, they luxuriated on immense chaises and piles of pillows, hookahs as tall as Christopher standing between them. Baskets sat beside them filled with the tiny smoking orbs, the creatures using small trowels to pour them into the hookah's wide bases.

Emi's eyes were wide and skittish, her head whipping around to take in everything she could. As her wonder grew, so did the tightening in Christopher's stomach. He rubbed the patch on his overalls, wondering how it was possible that he had knots in a stomach that was no longer there.

Before driving on through the market, the Huntress hopped down from her steed to drop curtains around their cages. Emi protested as they began to move once more, but her tantrums were lost in the squawking, roaring tumult of the city. There was much banging and clattering, some speech in languages both guttural and ethereal and, eventually, light as the curtains around their cages were pulled aside.

The Huntress was nowhere to be seen, nor her gruff

steed. They were somewhere inside one of the spires; a high monochrome sun glinted in through dark glass which made up the walls and floors. Although distant and warped, the movements of creatures in the street far below could still be seen if they peered downward. The Collectors hovered around them in the same loose formation, seemingly unaware of each other or of the room itself, only of Emi, sitting in her cage, picking the final stitches from the lace hem of her dress. She looked up, unperturbed by the limp corpses that floated around her.

"Welcome to the city of the Yokai, my friends."

From out of the shadows stepped a slender figure. A white robe lapped against its ankles as it strode forward. The shadows peeled back from the skull-like mouth and over the crest of a high head with a ruddy brown carapace. The creature's eyes were entirely white, but Christopher somehow knew when they were on him.

"I hear that you speak. Is this true?"

Christopher scowled, and willed Emi to stay quiet.

"Yes." Her voice came confident and clear, echoing back to them over and over.

The Collectors began to shudder collectively, the bony fingers on their flaccid hands trembling.

The slender creature clapped its long hands together.

"Remarkable," it laughed through lipless teeth. "Tell me everything. Tell me about yourselves. Tell me where you've been and what you've seen. Tell me about Old Earth. I'm particularly interested in the Sickness which caused your singular predicament. Tell me what you know… " The creature seemed to catch itself, tapping its teeth with its nails in frustration.

"You're monsters and you're going to eat us," Emi said, matter-of-fact.

The creature chuckled. "Monsters. How precious. Of course, we must seem as such. Especially these fellows behind me." He leaned forward so that only Emi could hear. "Even among our own kind, they're considered rather creepy." Then he stood tall once more. "I must apologise. How thoughtless of me. I was engrossed in my own fascinations. Allow me to make introductions. I am a student, if you will, of both the Old World and the one that remains. For they are quite different, as I'm sure you've noticed. I am Yokai, as you are human…"

"We aren't human anymore," Christopher said.

The creature seemed staggered. "Oh, I do apologise. I had no idea the term would cause offence. What would you prefer?"

Christopher looked at Emi, and fell silent.

"I'm Emi," said the little dead girl.

"Emi. Simplistic. Pleasing. And now, let me assure you that you are in no way at risk of being eaten. You are quite safe. In fact, the gentlemen behind me want nothing more than to ensure your continued existence. Now, that being said, there is a rather small matter of your leaving these halls. That is, you can't. But that is a small price to pay for your continued safety, I assure you."

"We're prisoners," Christopher said, to Emi in particular.

"Not at all, not at all. Think of yourselves as cherished exhibits. Let me show you."

Taking a large iron key from his robe, the Curator unlocked the sturdy padlocks on each cage and beckoned to them with long, fluid fingers. There seemed nowhere to go, until they walked toward him and, as their perspective shifted, entrances to the room became apparent in the carnival mirror walls. As they passed from one disorienting room to the other, the Collectors turned their veiled faces to follow their exit, but didn't move. To Christopher, they looked like priests with their sigils and vows of silence.

"Think of them as guardians," the Curator called back. "I have no idea why the term priest entered your head. Perhaps you had an aversion to them in the Old World?"

Christopher ignored the fact that his thoughts had been read. He was too busy pondering the Curator's words. Yes. Priests. Followers of a God. He had issue with them. But he couldn't remember why.

"I suspect you have forgotten much of what you once knew. Unlike those of the Yokai, mortal minds are not built to last. Not even in your undying state." He tapped his shell-like head with a click of a claw. "There is only so much capacity, if you prefer. Things may become half-remembered, or disappear entirely, otherwise you could learn nothing new. Hopefully what you can remember, you will share."

Emi placed her hand in Christopher's. He took it,

feeling a wave of some emotion come over him as his fingers wrapped around hers. He stared at the place where their fingers knotted together.

The Curator continued to chatter. "Yes. Memories. Tricky things. So much is forgotten, except the ones you can't forget. How does your mind choose which is which? A mystery."

In three neat rows down the centre of the next room, pillars, plinths and pedestals of clear glass held relics of Old Earth, things that set Christopher's mind afire with recognition. The first was a creature that he recognised: half of a man, its lower body in tatters, nothing left of its head but tendons leaving a neck, and trapped inside the glass cylinder.

"You have met this one before, I think. A shame it is in such terrible condition. Nothing like yourselves."

Emi seemed curious, but there was no flicker of acknowledgment for the creature she had crushed under her heel.

They passed a large beast, also frozen in glass, rectangular in body, horned, on four cloven feet. Where there had been a stomach was only a red, gaping hole. Christopher couldn't conjure a name for it.

"We found it after it and its brethren had been decimated by a clan of Kenku. It was possibly the last wild herd in existence. Sad. I would have liked to have dissected it myself."

Smaller glass columns displayed plants that Christopher hadn't seen in many centuries and, at the end of the room, were pedestals with shining chrome and white exhibits atop them.

"Your kind were fascinated with their technology," the Curator mused. Wandering between the exhibits, he seemed to have forgotten that he had companions, just muttering away to himself. "Favouring it over the natural miracles, it seems. Machines were made, rivers ran filthy, and so more machines were created to wash your clothing, clean your water, clean your bodies. Machines beget machines. A very odd species, were humans. And yet, at the end, many returned to the old ways. The old songs and stories all came back. Some of the old Gods felt things they hadn't in thousands of years. Belief. But only when all else had failed."

Emi was circling a two-wheeled machine, pale blue and chrome, perfectly preserved and maintained.

"What is it?" she asked.

"You ride it. It saves you from walking," Christopher said. He had tried one, once. He remembered the wind, the speed, the exhilaration.

"Can I try it?"

The Curator threw up his hands.

"Oh dear me, no. None of the exhibits are to be touched. Only preserved. Besides, the liquid required to make it work no longer exists. For which the World That Remains breathes a great sigh of relief. And now, let me show you where you will be staying. I hope you like it." The Curator pressed a sincere hand to his chest. "When we retrieved your carvings from the Nomad, we found that your needs were much simpler than if you were still alive. Still, I have provided seating, for the look of the thing. We do so want you to be comfortable here."

Another shift in perspective as they passed between rooms showed them a blank space, smaller than Emi's barn, with two wooden stools at its centre.

The Curator threw out his arms, each with more wrists than could possibly be useful.

"Welcome home!"

What sunlight filtered through the dark Yokai glass cast shifting patterns of deep blue and purple across the floor. Emi followed them around in little circles, the hem of her dress wafting outward as she spun in the darkest of colours. From the doorway, the Collectors observed, eyeless and unmoving other than the synchronised arcs of their heads as they watched her little dances and listened to her humming. Sometimes the Curator would bring her a bird or a beetle to play with.

They had stopped bothering with Christopher. He was in a mood. On the day that they arrived, he had sat with his gangly legs crossed in the centre of the room, ignoring the stools. His eyes became unfocused then and no amount of prodding from Emi or the Curator had made him move. The Collectors had been frustrated at first. They had gotten angry. They sent a hulking Yokai known as the Jaka to beat Christopher's flaccid body from wall to wall. But he was more stubborn than they could ever imagine and gave them no hint that he even knew they were there.

"He retains more human traits within him than he would have us believe," the Curator had said, leaning down to look into Christopher's eyes, which returned nothing. "In truth, although you are both quite spectacular, it is Emi with whom we are more fascinated. I think that there is some potential for experimentation if you aren't going to answer us, Christopher."

Still, nothing.

And so, the experiments began. Where the stools had once been, the Curator had installed a slab of Yokai glass atop which Christopher lay with arms outstretched and heels apart. The Curator circled him for the longest time, steepling his beetle-leg fingers in thought. Selecting a cruel pair of forceps from a glass pedestal which held several examples of poking and prodding paraphernalia, the Curator unhooked first one and then the other of the buttons which held Christopher's dungarees up by their straps.

Emi wandered over now, finally seeming to take interest in her companion's situation.

"I don't think he'd like you doing that," she offered.

"And yet he refuses to wake up to stop me."

"I don't think he's there when he gets like this. He goes for walks in his head."

"Then he won't know anything has been done at all."

She made a thoughtful sound as the Curator used the forceps to tug back the front flap of Christopher's clothing, the very one that he often absent-mindedly rubbed his hand across while thinking, peeling it back like opening a laboratory frog. Emi placed a hand to her own stomach, and found taut skin where Christopher had a hole. There beneath the ancient and stained denim, faint pink mixed with grey and dry as dust, Emi saw what the dungarees had been holding in. Not much. Without hesitation, the Curator began to pluck at the individual tendrils of what remained, lifting them out and setting them aside until Christopher lay surrounded by a bloom of his own tattered entrails.

Emi leaned right over to stare inside, poised on tiptoe to crane further.

"Is that what I'm like inside?"

"Yes," said the Curator, answering on reflex with his mind firmly delving in the cavity of his specimen.

"It doesn't feel like there's all that in there."

"I suppose it would be quite distracting if it did." The Curator's eyes finally rolled up toward the little dead girl. "This doesn't bother you?"

Emi regarded him, her little eyebrows without a whisper of thought or intent, yellow irises without even the calculation of a beast, never mind a human.

"I suppose not," the Curator commented, and returned to prodding the flaccid sack of Christopher's unused bladder with a long metal probe.

And, so far away that he might as well have been wandering among stars or the voids of the earth, Christopher gave them nothing.

The sun had risen hundreds of times since then.

Christopher remained unmoved. The Jaka had set him back in his place, positioning him like a doll so that he could be looked at, at least. Emi was scraping the remains of a centipede from the bottom of her foot as the rest twitched its mandibles before becoming still. She looked up to find the Curator squeezing between the archway to the room and the hanging Collectors.

"Good morning, Emi," he said. "Have you slept?"

"Not since last time," she said.

"And that was a time of great sadness for us. You were inert for several days. Quite the phenomenon that the Musician has created within you. An undying creature that requires no food or air, but sleeps. Quite peculiar, even in its infrequency." Bending his long spine so that his half-skull face was in line with Christopher's, he said, "Good morning, Christopher," and received the same lack of reaction that he always did.

"I played with my beetle," Emi said.

"I can see that. I wonder if any creature could survive you for long, little one." The Curator tussled her hair as he walked around the room, regarding the walls and the floor and the distant ceiling as if there was something of interest on the blank surfaces. "Do you remember anything else of the Old World, today?"

Emi shook her head and pointed to Christopher. "He remembers."

"Some things, yes. His carving was of great use to us. But his memory has limits. Some things his mind forgot with the heat of the Sickness. Some things he has forgotten on purpose. Such a shame. Alas, what shall we do today?"

Emi opened her mouth to answer, and an earth-deep rumble filled the room. Her eyebrows knotted, mirrored by the Curator, who stepped toward her, fascinated.

"How did you...?" But he was interrupted by another roar.

The Curator's hand lashed out to catch himself on a nearby wall as the room shook. Emi stumbled on the spot, managing to maintain her feet. Then came the sound, louder, closer, and not from the girl at all. A thunderous growl. In the doorway, the Collectors turned in unison and drifted away. The Curator's milky white eyes grew wide. Catching his balance, he rushed out past Emi, casting a swift look behind him to say, "Stay in your room."

Another quake. The tower shuddered. Christopher rocked on the spot. Emi stumbled again, arms outstretched to help her balance. Head cocked to one side, she moved toward the archway. In the exhibit hall, the clear pillars shook, their contents immovable inside. As Emi watched, one of the pillars snapped at the base, toppling toward a shattering end, chunks of glass and splattered entrails from the creature inside strewn across the floor. Another tremor. A section of the spire's wall shuddered, dropped a few inches, and then fell outward, the giant shard crashing down to the street below. She stepped out, up to where her little toes poked out over the hole's edge, wind whipping at her briar hair and soiled sundress. The streets below were full. All of the different shapes and colours of Yokai were surging in a single direction like rainbow water. As she searched back the way they had come, an immense form rounded another spire a little along the way. Twenty feet tall and coloured a deep red, the thing moved slowly but with purpose, groaning like a storm. She watched as it swung one powerful arm, and tiny motes went flying to the sound of screams.

More squawks and fearful ruckus turned her head away, where she saw another, this one a deep-sea blue. Raising its arms, hands melded into a single hammer, the giant creature slammed into the tower's base with an almighty force that knocked her clear off of her feet. She tottered, feeling herself pitch forward into the open air, to follow the shattered wall to the earth far below. For a second, her arms pinwheeled, her feet fighting to stay upright, and then the sensation was too sweet. The freedom of the air. And she opened her arms to feel what the birds felt.

She whip-cracked, her flaccid little body doubling over as she was yanked back. Christopher held her in one hand like a trophy, his face animated once more as he watched the carnage below.

"We have to leave."

Dragging Emi behind him, Christopher stalked through the exhibit room, ignoring the giant pillars as they split apart and crashed to the ground around him, stepping over debris with an easy stride. There was no sign of the Curator, or the Collectors. Through the room where they were unveiled and out the other side, a spiralling slope led down around the tower's hollow centre. Christopher didn't hesitate.

The next concussive blow sent him sprawling against the wall as a fault-line in the slope took this moment to crack and slide, sending tons of glass hurtling down into the spire, leaving a chasm where the floor had once been. Pressing his back to the wall, Christopher looked down at where his hand still wrapped Emi's as she dangled over the darkness, looking back at him. With one giant effort, he yanked her up toward him for the second time, scooping her bottom under his arm. Wrapping her arms and legs around him, she held on tight as he bunched his muscles for a leap. Sailing out over the chasm, Emi's bramble hair whipping out behind her, the darkness seemed to spread below, the gap widening as Christopher reached the peak of his leap and began to fall back down. The ground was still some way, the darkness opening up to claim them, until Christopher's feet slapped on the glass floor and he tumbled forward into a slide. Clutched together, they slid and then Christopher found his feet. Like a grasshopper, he cleared further broken sections of the slope in great lurching leaps, spiralling down and down to the foot of the spire as chunks of the construct fell from above and the thundering slam of the giant creature's fists continued to ring outside. All the while, Emi hung on.

As the slope reached ground level, Emi pointed a little finger away from the door that Christopher was heading toward, squirming to be put down. Pattering across the shaking ground, she bent over, hands on knees to regard what she'd found. The Curator sprawled on the ground, staring up into the spire's vault with his milky eyes, his lower half hidden beneath a jagged mountain of glass, ruined like the centipede she had played with earlier.

The Curator's mouth moved as if he was trying to speak, but there was no sound.

Emi looked over her shoulder to Christopher, who was hanging back.

The Curator continued to try, one insectile hand pawing weakly at the dead girl's skirts. Christopher's hand draped over Emi's shoulder, and the Yokai's head lilted to one side.

"We should go."

"Do you think that he was trying to say goodbye?"

"Perhaps. We should go."

Outside the spire's entrance, the Yokai swarmed or slithered, or fought their way into the air, always away from the footfalls which shook the ground. Now that Emi and Christopher were outside, the giant creatures' size could be appreciated more clearly. Powerful, rotund bodies pounded forward, masses of wild hair around their horned heads, eyes eager and bloodshot. Perching Emi on his hip, Christopher headed against the flow, toward the great beasts, hugging the spire's foundation as closely as he could. One swung a great club toward him, but he was faster, and the ground where he had been exploded in shards of earth as he landed elsewhere in a dead run. Around the spire and across another street, another of the giant creatures stood panting above a small Yokai on her knees in the dirt.

"Please, Oni-sama. Please let me go."

The Oni hurled its deep blue form forward, crushing the Yokai beneath its foot. Emi squealed with laughter before Christopher could slap a hand over her mouth. Parting its thick lips with a snarl, the Oni roared before breaking into a lumbering run in their direction. Christopher was already sprinting away, darting between the broken stalls and wagons of the market, leaping barricades with a single bound, his lithe arms pumping. Emi clung to his back now, a wild grin slathered across her face as she looked back toward the immense power of the Oni lumbering after them. Rounding another corner at speed, a group of small Yokai broke out of their hiding place, running on their hands, a fearful chittering filling the air, to swarm over the feet of the Oni, who groaned like a mountain as he swiped at them. The chittering ended in alarmed squeaks as the Oni crushed its prey, but the sound was lost to Emi and Christopher who were already a street away.

As they headed out to the meadow around the Yokai city, Christopher looked back just once as a glass spire toppled, smashing into its neighbour before falling into the rising dust cloud beneath. They continued away, pausing only to listen once more as the great scream of protesting metal rode the air. The brass tower fell with a final tone, a haunting aum that rang out over the horizon.

THE ROAD

The sound of the Yokai city's demise died away as the miles increased, booming Oni feet and wind-tossed screams fading into memory, the dust cloud settling as the horizon rose and rose. Out across the meadows they walked, Christopher with a terminal certainty, Emi zig-zagging between trees and plants and down to the banks of nearby streams. He never left her. And she never left. They were sometimes close and sometimes far away, but always together. They saw no Yokai in that time, heard no birds and only a few crawling creepies scuttled. The crunch of their feet became the loudest sound, tenacious nature the only sight.

It was at a time when the companions were near to each other, passing through a copse of trees, that Emi spotted the creature on Christopher's back. The hairy little imp clung to Christopher's overalls with overly large hands, its sloping face and upturned nose twitching as it spied at her.

"You have something on your back," Emi said, breaking a silence so long that Christopher had forgotten when it began.

"I know."

"Oh." She slowed down, looping around Christopher to get a better look.

The imp watched her with a suspicious squint.

"Hello," she said.

The creature sniffed the air toward her, but turned back to watch the road ahead from over Christopher's shoulder.

"What's your name?"

This time the imp shot her a frustrated look before returning to its clinging.

"I don't think it can talk," Emi said, once more walking beside Christopher.

"Maybe not," he replied, his brow furrowed. With that, he made his first stumble. The imp held on, its eyes wide, as Christopher maintained his feet.

"It's quite small," Emi commented.

"It weighs more than it should." His legs shook as he pushed himself upright once more, swaying backward slightly as he adjusted his balance to the creature's weight. "It's getting heavier."

"Tell it to go away," Emi offered.

"No. These things work in a certain way. I will carry it."

Soldiering on, Christopher was soon bent double beneath the hairy little creature that watched him with interest. His knees were beginning to quiver with each step, and twice he had to put his hands to the ground to stop from falling over.

Then, as they passed a large oak tree whose branches reached out over their path, Christopher shot upright at a thud behind him.

The creature was gone. Only a large hemp sack lay in the

road, tied at the neck with string. Untying it, Christopher revealed hundreds of small gold coins.

"What is it?" Emi plucked one from the top of the bag.

"Money."

"Shall we take it with us?"

"It isn't used for anything anymore," Christopher replied as he looked around for the little creature. Along the road in either direction, up into the branches of the old oak. It was gone.

Emi tucked the gold piece into the little pocket in her dress that she used for colourful rocks, shiny beetle shells and shards of bone. Christopher looked down at the bag for another moment before following her.

Where a river widened to an estuary, the waters becoming sluggish in their old age before release to the sea, an old dinosaur skeleton of a bridge stretched across the waters, scratching the sky with its warped bones. Stubborn infant trees had found a little root to grow somewhere in the splintered road surface. Hung on thick threads from the underside, dark green sacs swung and twisted their bulbous forms in the breeze. Christopher eyed them for a while, but could see no movement in them.

Emi had found one of the great iron stanchions and began balancing along its length as it climbed, her arms waving for stability, feet dwarfed by the slumbering heads of large iron bolts that ran in rows along its length. Christopher followed. Up the steady slope, crisscrossing between broken sections of road, they made their way through the sparse and brittle copse of bridge trees.

The sound came first, a wet creaking sound like the shrinking of swamp wood. Then the thick, sweet scent of fresh bile rose in the air. Christopher turned slowly around, taking in the sky and the naked, introvert trees. He spun full circle until he came back to Emi, who had stopped a little way ahead, now in the middle of the road, and was looking back at him.

Their hands came first, like twigs knotted together with string, reaching over the bridge's sides to take purchase on the steel, dragging after them the spider-like limbs and hairy, moss-ball bodies. Without eyes or mouths, it was impossible to tell which way they were facing, or if angry or hungry or sad.

Christopher watched as the creatures scuttled atop the bridge and then down, more and more of them, and none any larger than Emi herself. Emi gazed upon them with her usual level of candour, until they drew closer. As the swarm swelled, forming a rippling sea of wet green bodies, Emi threw out her arms. As one, the creatures surged back by a few feet, and froze. Emi's laugh fell like glass. Christopher watched, head cocked, as the little girl turned slowly in a circle. Then, with arms curled outward, legs bent and back hunched, she puffed out her cheeks and lowered her brow. Stamping her feet around in a circle, Emi played the part of an Oni, grumbling sounds that she had heard but couldn't possibly understand, growling like thunder.

The creatures watched her.

"Raaaarrrr," Emi yelled, and the creatures scattered, skittering away like tossed gravel, back over the bridge's sides in a flurry of green bodies and spidery limbs.

Pleased with herself, Emi dusted her hands, and went back to playing her game.

Christopher watched her go for a while, and then followed.

The hedges and forests fell away, swift streams grew into rivers, swollen and slow in their adolescence. Where hills had once been, now vast open plains of sickly grass danced on a salty breeze. Every night, when the moon rose, off to one side of the road where the grass grew in stiff clumps and the earth was scarred with rivets and holes that cast pockmark shadows, little blue flames floated down from the air, coming to rest like seeds of greater fires to come, and by sunrise they would dwindle and die. Every night they came and every morning they winked out. As the fields also fell behind, so did the little flames, and Emi and Christopher never saw their like again.

The breeze grew and grew, tightening Christopher's skin even more than it already was with the briny mist that it carried. As the Yokai city slipped from their minds entirely, their feet brought them to the edge of a crumbling cliff which dived down into a surging grey sea. Dropping to her belly, Emi lay with her head and arms dangling over the edge to watch foamy wave crests draw together in heaves, surging forward to sacrifice themselves on the rocks for the sake of flight. Emi's tallow, grinning face caught the mist, and sent her laughter back down to the rumbling ocean.

Christopher wandered away, returning a while later to find her still laughing at the sea.

"I've found something."

The something was a stout tower on the cliff's edge, beaten by weather and sprouting weeds between its stones. Christopher pushed a heavy metal door at its base, the rusted hinges giving way, throwing down the door with a clatter which sent a plume of birds scattering from the tower's summit. In the darkness, a darker shape could be seen, a helix of iron steps reaching upward.

Christopher peered up into the vault, saw nothing of interest, and made to leave but jerked to a stop when Emi's little hand clasped the edge of his dungarees.

"Let's look."

They climbed. In places where the steps had shunted free of the wall, they inched sideways along the stanchions and rails. Spiders hissed in the dark, stamping their feet and scuttling between shadows in a wary dance. Step by step and metre by metre they made their way up toward the top of the tower where an unlocked trapdoor clattered onto the upper floor's boards. Filthy beyond belief, yellowed by age and half-blind with spider web cataracts, the great glass window that encircled the tower's summit let only a hint of light leak in. With her little hand, Emi began to scrape away at the dirt of the window, making no headway at all. The dirt was too old and stubborn. Scrunching up her nose, she wandered the circuitous walkway, coming back to Christopher.

"There's nothing here."

"You expected something more?"

"I suppose not." Staring out through the murky glass, she sighed. "What is that over there?"

"That's the sea. There's just more of it and then more of this."

"We should go there."

"Why?"

"We should go."

Christopher looked down at her, then out across the undulating slate sea. "Alright."

Walking along the clifftop, they came to a place where a rocky slope carried them down to a shale beach. Their bare feet making crunching progress across the stones, they walked toward the sea, unperturbed by the lapping of the grey waters. Not when it caressed their ankles, not when it covered their knees, not when the cold sea claimed their stomachs or their chests, and not bothering to close their eyes or hold breath they wouldn't need, they disappeared beneath the waves.

BENEATH THE WAVES

At first, sunlight leaked from above in shattered spotlights that cast hasty beams around them. The soft, wet sand sucked at their feet and the tide tugged at their hair. Emi, in particular, looked like a travelling coral reef with her golden hair in an aura around her head. Tiny silver-blue fish found her first, darting in and out of her locks, looking for food that wasn't there. She reached up to touch them but, lucky for them, they were too swift. Christopher strode on, his steps longer, dragged slower by the pull of the sea. They walked and walked until the light faded from above completely, leaving them in a murky world that gave no hint of passing days, no celestial markers, eating time as surely as light. Fish and eels darted out of the dark and then flashed away, or writhed around them in tingling bands. Through the heavy sand, rocks began to thrust upward, at first smaller, and then larger and larger, climbing higher and higher until the valleys and crevasses they made were as large as anything on land.

Emi opened her mouth to express how similar this was to the dry parts of the world, but nothing came out. Not even a bubble. Christopher watched her try to speak, watched her little face become confused and then accepting. There were no sensations of wind or movement when the sea was pressed against every part of his body. The water around him stole any sound away, any light. He stopped, closed his eyes for a second, and listened to the blessed nothing.

His hand jerked. Emi stood below him tugging at it, as she always did. If he could have sighed, he would. They walked on together.

As the darkness enveloped them, Christopher led the way with one arm outstretched before him. The ground led ever down and down, the sand giving way to slivers between the layers of stone, slick with dancing green fronds. The rocks ended suddenly, and the companions stepped out onto a thin ledge, the drop before them a sucking darkness. Christopher held out a hand to stop Emi toppling over.

There. Out in the dark was a sound. The first they'd heard. A mournful wail, the creak of a breaking soul. They felt it in their chests, their heads alive with the sound as it wrapped around them and, in the darkness, a spark of light, gone as soon as it came. Then again, over to their right. A pulse, then it was gone. Christopher swayed back on his heels as the sea before them was suddenly filled with a great mass. Surging past them, it let out another groan that could shatter glass, and its body, from snub nose to immense tail, pulsed in a wave of bright white as if it were passing through a hoop of divine light. It dove down, down into the chasm before them, the last swoop of its tail churning the waters. Then another pulse of light, far off, deep down, and the sorrow song died away.

Smothered in darkness once more, Christopher led

them along the crevasse edge. It was that or climb down into the dark. The chasm below grew no less imposing and the sea no less dark and the rocky cliff to their side no less impenetrable. Until Christopher spotted an outcropping of the cliff ahead, a place where some spike of stone had crumbled over the centuries and come to its final rest horizontally, reaching out into the darkness across the crevasse.

Taking Emi's hand, he led her up the slope of crumbled stone and sand that had collected at its base, onto the top of the fallen pillar, and out across it. The chasm wasn't as wide as he had assumed and it took almost no time at all to cross the rock bridge, feeling their way.

The sea bed opened up to them once more and they traversed in the darkness for untold time until the ground began to rise before them. The rocks pulled away and the sand returned, shoals of fish broke around them in bursts of silver scales. In a moment like any other, as the pair traipsed through the murk, the water above them grew light, the sun returned, and the crowns of their heads broke the surf, wading up onto a vast swathe of wind-tossed sand.

THE GUIDE

Emi mused that this side of the ocean looked very much the same as the other. There were rivers and forests, there were old roads and crumbled stones where people had once lived. Until, where the meadows met the mountains, grassy hills became grey earth and Christopher and Emi climbed upward. Emi's interest was piqued once more. Wide valleys carved their way through the land as they climbed up and up toward the mountains. Veils of mist obscured odd creatures that occasionally stalked, sometimes behind and sometimes ahead, with thick, swaying bodies and withered arms, the occasional flash of a wide and unforgiving mouth. But they never drew close and Christopher paid them little mind. Where the mountains truly took hold, the snow came in large flakes which turned to blinding walls of freezing air. Trying to find their way through walls of stone and across crumbling ledges, they fought on with Christopher making trenches through the tundra with his long limbs for Emi to follow. Despite the biting wind, neither Emi nor Christopher grumbled about the cold. It wasn't until their joints began to creak and groan as they moved that their progress slowed.

Emi tried to speak, to ask what was happening, but her jaw was solid. She creaked her head up to see that

Christopher's skin had lost its tallow hue and was now the pale blue of icicle skies. Frost had crept its way across his unmoving cheek and brow to decorate him with glistening fingers. He moved only in jerks, sometimes rocking on the spot as he fought against the freeze until… he didn't.

On a high mountain pass with the crystalline sun above and the snow building all around, Emi looked at Christopher and Christopher looked at Emi, unmoving, until the snow filled the space between them, also, and there was only white.

Realising that he had nothing to do but wait for the thawing of spring, Christopher turned his mind inward.

Where were they going? That is what everything wanted to know. Where. The destination. Where would it be? Where was he taking the thing that had been a girl? Where was he taking himself? Christopher's mind wandered, trying to conjure an alien concept that wouldn't come. The end. To stop. A place to be. Surely that was a thing for mortal creatures. For him, there was no need to find comfort or warmth, to rest or to eat, and he had nothing to keep. Nothing to stow or store. Nor did he need a place where he could be found. Anyone who wanted to find him was gone and gone again.

Images coalesced from the darkness as he thought, half formed and misty, rushing like spectres that merged with him and then were gone. Rooms, faces, snatches of babble. The tastes were the worst. The need to put something into his mouth to maintain his existence was a distant ember in the dark that seemed arbitrary to the creature he had become. Smoke. He remembered the crisp black coating on charred meat. Huddling around a flame to cook. The swirls of sound, like water mixed with the cawing of birds. Laughter and sunshine. A garden. His. Grass kept prisoner by a wooden fence. A dirty apron where he wiped his hands. Children and their tamers. Skipping and dancing and screeching, a dizzying blend of shattering sound and pastel colours. Hair like chestnut. Eyes of the deep ocean green. The rest fell away as her smile turned from where it was aimed and then passed by him, so that he could almost believe that it was all his. Dimpled knees and dimpled cheeks. Beauty that deserved to last forever, that age would steal away. Unless he saved her. Tears. Damp concrete and blankets. Cardboard books with scuffed edges and faded pictures. A doll with woollen hair, friend to many that it had outlived. Stories in the dark, quiet at first, but louder and louder to drown out the pleading for home.

Buried in the snow, Christopher twitched despite himself as a door hammered and the voices of men cut the air of his refuge. The slam of his chest against the hollow metal of a car's bonnet. Flaring blue and jangling silver. And over the houses, the thunder of an explosion, the roar fading to reveal screams buried beneath. Hundreds of people stampeding toward him, for him, after him, he was sure, but past and then gone, leaving only the blood-stained and moaning masses that pierced and tore as he lay discarded, forgotten and helpless. And the world ended.

"Deardeardeardeardear. Poor souls. Poor poor souls."

Christopher became aware of the voice first, the scraping sound of earth, then of movement. But it wasn't his own. He wasn't moving at all. As he came back to his eyes, he found himself staring at a vast expanse of blue, wisps of frosty cloud scudding across it. In halting drags, he was being borne on a wooden frame along the mountain pass. The snow was gone, the mountain's craggy sides rose all around, and Emi laid across his chest like a piece of lumber.

"So cold out here, so dangerous. Poor silly souls," the dusty voice chuntered on.

Christopher tested his limbs. There was a little give. His smaller joints, fingers and toes, were bouncy. He would be able to use them soon. His knees and elbows were another story entirely. His face was still stiff.

After a while, the sky disappeared, replaced by the rocky roof of a cave. Stone knives jabbed down at him, out of the dark. Tiny eyes of the creatures that roosted there, judging silently. With ropes wrapped around his head and shoulders, Christopher was hoisted upright, swung on his heels like an old wardrobe, and propped in a corner.

The cave was small, almost circular, with a day-lit tunnel to one side and a darker one to the other. He watched the little man scuttle back and forth with his long grey robe flapping, gathering wood into a peak and lighting it with the spark of a tinderbox held in hands with too few fingers to match the too few toes on his pale feet. Two wispy growths, only a few hairs thick, sprouted from beneath his nose and dangled down to his chest. A matching pair cascaded from his ears. The cave danced in the firelight as the little man sat and stared into the flames, humming to himself, and Christopher could finally see clearly what had been evading his understanding. What he had first thought to be a smudge of dirt on the little man's bald scalp was, in fact, a very smooth-edged hole with darkness inside. Surely another Yokai, although unlike any he had ever seen.

In time, when the heat had done its work, Christopher creaked his head around to look for Emi and found her on the opposite side of the fire, laid out with the steam of melting frost rising from her.

The little man gave a raven-like exclamation.

"Ackh!"

Christopher's head swung about until he regarded the little man, who had fallen back from the log he was perched on, his eyes wide as he looked at Christopher.

"Alive! By the stars, he's alive."

"No," Christopher croaked. "Not quite. But it's a common mistake."

"Not dead. Not alive."

"That's right." With great effort, Christopher creaked forward at the waist. When his weight shifted to the point of toppling, he snapped out one leg to catch himself. With each movement it became a little easier. His joints groaned him down to sit by the fire, across from the little man who watched with wide, watery eyes.

"You rescued us," Christopher said.

The little man shook his head, whiskers swishing. Christopher couldn't take his eye from the skull hole.

"Not rescuing," croaked the Yokai. "You don't rescue dead folks, or so I thought."

"And you bring dead things here for what reason?"

"Better than leaving them out there. There are hungry things out there. Imagine if you'd have woken with yourself half chewed!"

Christopher shrugged.

"You are going through the mountains?" The little man cawed.

With a nod, Christopher waited for the question. *Where?* But it never came.

"Then you go down, not up. I will show you the way." A large-knuckled finger pointed to the darker tunnel opposite the cave's entrance. "Down and down and on and on. And then up to the sunlight again. The mountain roads are too cold for you, it seems."

Looking over his shoulder, Christopher regarded the deep darkness, then Emi.

"Is it safe?"

"No," croaked the little man.

Christopher nodded. "Alright."

Having fallen into one of her sleeping epochs while frozen, it took a while longer for Emi to wake. The little man ate dried shards of meat from his pockets and sipped a hot liquid from a cracked ceramic bowl too hot to hold so that he had to keep setting it in his lap to blow on his fingers. But, once Emi finally woke and had made herself acquainted with their new guide, they were all ready for the journey. The little man lit a long match from the fire and, shielding it with his other hand, led the way to the cave's rear.

The ground sloped downward, slowly at first and then all at once, into a tunnel where daylight would soon be forgotten. From an alcove cut into the rock, their guide produced a bundle of long white candles. Selecting one and pocketing the rest, he inserted it into the hole in his head, gave it a twist, and lit it with the taper. Emi watched with fascination as the light spread around the Guide's head in a golden corona, bringing light to the confining stone around them, and even giggled when he smiled at her and the same golden light poured from between his uneven teeth.

Down and down they went, the slope becoming a ledge that skimmed the outer edge of a great chasm filled with darkness that seemed to breathe, dragging air down into its vastness, tugging at clothing and hair. When their feet sent crumbling rock over the edges, there was only silence as the stones fell from the light.

"I'm sure I don't have to tell you to be careful here," the Guide said. "If you were to fall here, you might fall forever. Perhaps right through the world, out the other side, and into the sky." He chuckled. "Or you might not, of course. No one really knows."

Christopher looked to Emi, who was taking little precaution while leaning over to stare into the abyss. He had carried on moving and thought, as she fell behind, that if she were to go over the edge, he wouldn't be close enough to catch her. He thought to say something, but didn't, only keeping moving and watching every now and again. Eventually she came back to the safety of the ledge and made her way after them.

Christopher sighed, a strange thing as he didn't usually bother to breathe at all.

The ledge dove back into the mountain's roots, taking them with it. The walls became rougher, and moist in places so that long tendrils of moss crept and merged along the walls, the moisture glistening in the Guide's light. A sound came to them, a distant chugging that grew as they went, and the smell of charred coal and heat.

"Don't be afraid. He is a friend. Or was," the Guide said.

"We're not," both companions replied in unison.

In time the three travellers reached a place where the tunnel split into two.

"This is not our way, but you might like to see. Come along."

The Guide took them off the main tunnel, down one half its height and less finely crafted. Thick black smoke billowed along the ceiling, seeking the open air. In a short while they came to regard the back of some other creature. A black iron funnel belched smoke, its other end attached to the creature at a metal band around its waist which was decorated with small vents that showed the glow of embers inside. The creature scratched at the tunnel's blind end with huge spade-like hands, sending rock tumbling to its feet.

"He doesn't talk anymore. We used to take tea together and talk of all of the things beneath the earth. But that was a long time since. Now, all he can do is dig and dig. All his energy, spent to find more energy." The Guide shook his head.

Then, the clattering of steel on stone stopped. Only the chugging remained.

The creature hunched down with a long, dry wheeze, scooping something from the ground and holding it to the lantern that hung over its back. They could see its face a little, a blunt stub smeared with black and cranberry eyes that blinked against the weak light. It paid them no mind, although surely it knew they were there. A small black rock clutched between its fingers. Opening a grate in its stomach that spat orange embers, the creature tossed the tiny rock inside, and closed the grate before returning to its dauntless and noisy task.

"As I said," the Guide muttered, solemnly. "Someday I will surely find him all out of puff. Staring at that wall with his lantern snuffed. It will be a sad day. But on we go. Let's leave our friend to his work."

The Guide slowed his pace as they continued, his feet growing heavier, breath laboured, one hand reached out to the damp wall. Candle after candle lived and died, wax cooling in long dribbles down his face and back to break off as he mopped his brow. As the last candle died, Christopher expected them to be pitched into darkness. He thought of Emi behind him and of how there were no other tunnels, no other turns to take. Perhaps if there had been, she would have become lost beneath the earth. But there was no darkness as a cold green glow came from up ahead, giving the Guide's silhouette an eerie aura.

"Ah, here we can rest," he said with panting words as the tunnel opened into a great chamber.

Emi stepped out into the full force of the glow, her little eyes growing wide as she looked around.

A forest. Towering mushrooms crawled their way toward an unseen ceiling; toadstools that could shade a Gaum, their trunks curved and wavering, their tops spreading out in vibrant umbrellas which shed the eerie green glow. Bearded tendrils hung with moss that wafted in some subterranean breeze.

The Guide led on into the forest without pause, his footfalls heavy on the dirt. Where a clump of smaller mushrooms sprouted from the bedrock in a pale explosion, a small wooden hut sat lopsided and forlorn. The Guide stumbled inside as Emi and Christopher watched.

"It's small, but you're welcome," he said, barely finding the energy to express the sounds.

Christopher leaned to see. The hut had one rickety bunk, and enough floor space to get in and out. That was all.

"We don't need sleep. We'll wait outside," said Christopher.

With each nod, the Guide's head became heavier and heavier until it struggled to rise at all. "Don't wander too far. I might not find you again," he said, as the hut's door closed. Christopher swore that he heard a thump from inside as the Guide's slumbering body hit the bunk.

Christopher sat to wait, hands on his worn knees, as Emi wandered out among the mushrooms, washed in pale green fluorescence. Allowing his eyes to unfocus, she was lost among the ambient glow.

When the Guide awoke, he gathered his things which included a handful of candles from a box beneath the bunk, and found his dead companions sitting quietly outside.

"Off we go!"

Christopher and Emi trailed after him as he led on through the mushroom forest, over creeping fungi tendrils and through copses of curled and curious toadstools. The tunnel at the other side of the cavern was much the same as the one before, still sloping down, still slick and hard. Every now and then they would pass another of the Guide's little huts and he would rest and replenish his candles. The rocks around them grew drier, the scent that they didn't realise they had been smelling all along, the rich smell of fresh soil, died away and was replaced by, at first, simply a dry absence of anything, and then the growing rotten smell of the deep earth. Emi wrinkled her nose at it, which was why Christopher noticed it at all.

"Why are you doing that?" he asked.

"The smell isn't very nice."

He breathed in through his nose, sucking up the scent, and felt his own face shrink and cluster at the smell. And then he realised why she had smelled it and not him.

"Have you been breathing this whole time?"

She turned her neat little chin up to him quizzically.

"Only sometimes. Don't you?"

"No. You don't have to."

"I know. It just feels nice."

And that was that. Christopher chose not to smell the smell anymore, although it took a while for the lung-full he had breathed to lose its potency, and Emi must have done the same because her face eventually relaxed as well. The Guide seemed unperturbed by it at all.

Soon the source of the smell became evident as the rock passages opened up to reveal subterranean rivers of oozing red and orange glow, slick black pools spreading on its bubbling surface, the air above it hazy with heat and the rotten gas. The lava flowed along, and fell from the chasm above; it spat and it surged. Christopher could feel his already dry skin pricking at the heat of it, small tendrils of smoke rising from him here and there. Emi's hair in particular was parched and sizzling, the tips curling like withering limbs. Their faces and clothing were soon coated in a fine ash.

"The earth is still young, deep down where it counts," the Guide said. "No matter how the continents shift or creatures come and go, down here it's still hot, still has its old power."

The Guide led on.

In time the earth rose again, the heat peeled back from them, and the ground became something else. Christopher felt the thud of wood beneath his feet as slats rose from the earth, evenly spread and joined by iron bars at either side. Emi was playing some game where the ground could no longer be touched, forcing her to jump from plank to plank, arms spread wide for balance as she hopped after him. He tried to remember what the bars were for. He knew once, he was certain of that, but it just wouldn't come.

"These things," he addressed the Guide. "Do you know what they are?"

"I believe they are called… rails," the little man called back from a little ahead, pronouncing the alien word carefully. "Made for moving large things back and forth beneath the ground. Humans were very clever, except for where it counted."

"Where was that?" Emi asked, now hoppity hopping with both dirty feet at once.

"I'm sorry?"

"Where did it count?"

The Guide slowed to regard her as the girl's jumps caught her up to him and then carried her right past, her eyes not leaving her game. He looked to Christopher who shrugged like a glacier.

"In matters of the heart, mostly," the Guide said, following the girl into the dark. "Humans always chose the mind and the self, forgetting the difference between

119

can and should. Whipped their Mother Earth into slavery..." He prodded the rails with a toe. "...shackled her with iron and burnt her blood. How else was it ever going to end?"

"Some people were grateful for it when it came. The end," Christopher muttered, seemingly unaware of his own voice.

"Some people were smarter than others. Good manners say that you must always know when you've outstayed your welcome." The Guide became aware that the girl wasn't even listening anymore. Had she ever? Her game was far more important to her.

The rails guided them on through further stone corridors that now steadily climbed, sometimes splitting where a rusted mechanism would have changed the flow of whatever pushed along them. Where such a dilemma presented itself, the Guide led on with confidence. Soon, there was light ahead that spread its arms to welcome them to the world above once more.

ABOVE

The last they saw of the Guide, he was sitting around a fresh fire, scooping the old wax from the hole in his head, gnawing on a piece of dry meat and counting his candles. He waved them goodbye, his grin spreading too many wrinkles on too small a face before turning back to his task.

Standing at the far edge of the range, the land spread out below them. Gone was the green, the treetops and meadows. Instead, where the mountains worked their roots into the earth was a sparse grassland of parched yellow and dry beige. The air hung like dust, a faint breeze simply moving the soft heat around.

They headed down into it.

Fragile fronds spread around them, scratching at exposed, insensitive skin and tugging at clothing, making the companions' progress halted and staggering. Birds sat in the wide and naked branches of solitary trees in droves, staring. Insects either tumbled drunkenly under glossy shells or hummed in hovering miasmas.

It was by moonlight, wandering through the wastes, that they heard the first crunch of earth, far off. A tree-like groan was returned by another in some lowly call and answer, and the sound of slow trampling grew near.

Christopher and Emi stood in the dark, their golden hair and golden eyes standing out like the deep-earth mushrooms, and watched the herd pass by.

Twice a Gaum in height, their skin the colour of grey soil, the beasts groaned as they walked with leaden feet that hung with roots beneath. Small-snouted heads hung low as if leading their expansive bodies by the neck, their eyes tucked under a wide crenulation. Emi craned her neck, almost falling backward in the effort to see that, on their backs, the beasts wore great hanging gardens. Trees, wide and flat, flowering vines that clung to the beast's flanks, blossoms like outstretched hands that led down into deep funnels that sprouted pale tongues, all worn by the beasts like a caparison and washed into shades of black and silver by the moonlight.

They watched, as the night wore on and the moon dipped, until the herd had passed into a faint sound at the edge of hearing and, as the sun rose, only a hint of rising dust showed their spot in the distance.

Sand churned the air in intertwined maelstroms that fought for ownership of Christopher and Emi, dragging them by the arm, the leg, the hair, blind and buffeted. Even Christopher had thrown one arm over his eyes to stop the battering grains from filling his eyes and mouth until he could no longer close them. Emi was a vague weight behind him as he fought on and on. There was a hint of sunlight, or rising and falling light beyond the storm, but only as the difference between complete, razor-filled darkness and a scything amber tempest.

Once, where some eye opened in the storm, off to one side, Christopher swore he saw a towering shape, a single black finger in the desert, its uppermost end seeming to scratch at the belly of the sun. And although it had been untold ages since he had seen anything else, he had no desire to go there, grateful that Emi didn't see and demand that they change direction.

With time that seemed longer than they had ever known, they passed beyond the storm and could look back on it. From this side, the tower was nowhere to be seen, and Christopher allowed himself a sigh. They stood for some time, Christopher releasing the flap of his dungarees to let the sand empty from the cavity beneath, and Emi bent double to let the sand pour from inside her where she had not thought to keep her mouth closed. As she stood up, wiping the last of the grains from her cracked pout, he finally looked at her. All of the dirt and grease on the little dead girl had melded with the wind and her hair. That golden thicket that could pass as part of the desert if she would only lay down, the thing that he had seen first of her, stood back from her like an outcrop.

The sensation fluttered inside him first, deep in his stomach where there was nothing to flutter. Then it rose into his chest to become a spasm. His shoulders shook, just once, and then again. He unleashed an odd bark that startled as much as it fascinated.

Emi stood like a half-blown dandelion, her little

face pasted in sand, yellow eyes wide and curiously expressionless, and said, "What's wrong?"

Christopher's laugh exploded.

It shook and it roared, it ebbed and flowed, and every time he looked at the little dead girl with the mussed-up hair, it reared like a stallion once more. He let it come as if he had any choice in the matter, marvelling as his body was rocked, as he doubled over to wrap his arms around his stomach, as he slapped his leg and wrapped a hand around his own mouth, as his face, stretched into a rictus of mirth, expressed the line between pain and glee, and as tears, drawn from some stagnant well deep down inside him, rose to his eyes and fell to the hungry ground.

Somewhere in the middle of that dry earth, far from sea and storm, where the paths of beasts had no cause to go, was where they found the village. It appeared from the desert's heatwaves as a dream, only becoming a reality when the coarse thatch rooftops coalesced into view. Then there came the top of a stout tree complete with dark leaves, and then a narrow post wrapped with colourful strips of cloth and string that fluttered in the breeze.

Christopher and Emi approached, as dauntless as they had begun, stopping only when a wavering form approached through the heat-haze.

Tall as Christopher, with taut brown skin, mid-length hair held back with a little row of medallions, the man stood lithe and graceful. He held a staff of his own height

although he didn't need it to stand, his body swathed in a single wrap of red fabric, and a line of three thumb-sized white marks beneath his right eye. The man stopped a few feet short of them, regarding each of them casually in turn.

Christopher's eyes grew wide and unblinking. He scanned the symmetrical form up and down, over and over as if nodding to himself. He counted fingers and toes, he noted the position of nostrils and eyebrows. Not a scale or a horn or a tail was to be found.

When the man was done exchanging cursory glances, he turned back toward the village. A little way off, he turned to see if they were following and, when they weren't, seemed to wait for them to do so.

Emi was looking up at Christopher, her eyebrows crushed in incomprehension.

"I don't understand," she said.

Christopher just shook his head, and started walking after the man. When Emi followed, the stranger continued leading the way.

THE VILLAGE

The closer they came to the village the more dreamlike it became. Christopher's mind was a wash of fragmented memories, overlaid on the village until he couldn't be sure which was real and which a past-life image. The huts with their straw roofs, sack-hung doorways and naked apertures made a natural row that led into the heart of the village. Christopher remembered a street, brick facades and squares of glass, window boxes in bloom, and over that, another layer of burnt husks, the sound of fearful panting, footfalls, the scent of old meat and taste of copper.

The red-wrapped man led on, his staff making little huffs in the dust. Where the village opened up into a clearing, he walked across a wooden grid, half covered in sand and dirt. At the other side, he stopped, and turned to them once more.

Emi sauntered on, unawares, until Christopher clapped a hand on her shoulder as her toes reached the edge of the grid. She looked up at him.

"What's wrong?"

Christopher searched around. The grid was cross-shaped, and he could now see the ropes that stretched away from the frame, disappearing into doorways around the square.

"It's a trap. A box," he said.

"Are they bad people?"

"Not necessarily."

At that, the red-wrapped man's face widened in surprise. He stepped back, uncertain, switching glances between the dead man and the little girl. Finally, he spoke, slowly, clearly, casting words like an inquisitive fishing line.

Neither Christopher nor Emi understood them.

Christopher shook his head.

"We don't understand you."

The man shook his head, said something else. Still no understanding passed between them. Turning his head, he passed a comment toward one of the huts where a wizened woman stepped out of the shadows. Her skin was the same rich brown as the man, although creased like sun-dried fruit. A knitted wrap that hung around her shoulders swung down by her knees as she waddled forward, under her own steam but only just. With one tree-root hand, she waved the red-wrapped man aside.

Still remaining on the opposite side of the grid, she regarded the new arrivals with oyster-like eyes, greying at the corneas. She spoke words, her eyes growing narrow as Emi and Christopher looked at each other, and then raised her voice, throwing it over her shoulder. In the various doorways and from around the corners of huts, people began to emerge. All dark skinned, all dressed in varieties of colour and style, trousers and skirts, topless and enrobed, some painted with dots and stripes on their limbs and some not. Christopher looked, and his memory tried to place these people. But there was too much of too many for a definitive answer. No one skin tone or material colour or style of dress led to anything of the Old World. At the end of the wide world, what was left had become these people. That was all he could presume.

At one side of a serpentine bonfire sat the dead, at the other, cast in wary shadows, the living. Christopher sat with legs crossed and hands on his knees, Emi with her threadbare skirts spread around her.

"You said everyone was gone."

"I thought it was true."

"How are they here?"

"They could have walked. That's how we got here."

"How long have they been here?"

"Perhaps the whole time."

"You said you'd walked everywhere."

"I was wrong."

And so, the conversation on one side of the fire went around in loops and leaps of logic. At the other side, there was mostly silence and eyes reflecting the firelight, never leaving the unliving spectacle as the tribe ate from earthenware bowls with their fingers. When the eating was done, the people danced and sang. Haunting and powerful, their voices rose up into the void of the night, their feet drawing curlicues in the sand as they danced, some in pairs, hands held and bodies close, others alone kicking the dirt with arms stretched wide. It was hard not to see the stars in them, each a shape in the great wheel of constellations.

The night drew on and Yng, the moon-bearer, climbed wearily to his bed beyond the horizon, his bag of water half full. Emi thought that he had done a good job tonight. The people wandered away, one by one, until only the old woman and one man remained. Speaking briefly to him, she too wandered away to her own hut. The man wrapped himself in a coarse blanket, and remained. Christopher and Emi watched him, and he watched them. They watched as his head began to nod, his blinks growing longer and longer, and then his head snapping up as he stared around himself hurriedly. He would spot them, still sitting where they had been, and he would calm again, the process going around and around until the sky grew light and the people returned.

That was how Christopher and Emi spent their first day in the village.

Christopher sat. He found a spot in the village's open centre that people rarely needed to walk through so that he was out of the way but could watch. He watched them by day and by night, by sun and by firelight, as they lived their lives. He didn't retreat into his memory anymore. Instead, the images came to him, overlaying the villagers with people in overcoats, carrying rustling plastic bags or pushing carts with children in them. Once, he jerked to his feet as a speeding blue car hurtled through the village, heading to cut down the villagers, but passed right through. Sometimes burning hulks would appear where the bonfire had once been. The villagers didn't see any of it. The old woman would come to him with bowls of water and he would wash the dust from himself, and then she stopped coming and a younger woman with a similar face brought the water.

Emi played with the children. Now that Christopher saw her with them, how she moved and acted, in dips and skips and flights, made sense to him. The young ones and the little dead girl swirled around each other like stew lumps in a stirred pot, screeching in a way that at first had the adults running, but became less and less. They grew taller around her, a thorn bush surrounded by pines, and she would sit with him a while until there were new children to play with.

He wasn't certain how long passed, but soon there were no faces left of the ones that had watched him and Emi through the fire that first night. And when the final night came, he knew none of the voices that screamed and screamed and screamed.

FLAME

There was already nothing for it. He knew. The single well that fed the village would never be enough to cut down the forest of flame that had sprouted up beneath the village and already stretched its flickering branches higher than the rooftops.

This was an end. And he was as powerless now as he had been the last time he'd witness one. When he tried to stand, it was a struggle. It had been so long since he'd done it that his bones complained, but he didn't listen. He wandered through the burning village as roofs groaned and crumbled, as clay cracked and as the villagers became shadows at the centre of the flames. In the street, he found one or two of them, unburnt, but gone none-the-less. He made circles through the writhing conflagration, stared up as embers spun like fresh stars against the night sky.

In time, he found what he knew he would find.

Emi stood with her tallow face and wide, yellow eyes staring into the flames. Her feet and legs were dark from the stamping, hands dirty with her night's work, dress sooty and almost indistinguishable from the night around her.

"Why?" he asked. There was nothing else to say.

"They keep growing up. I want them to stop. I wanted them to be small and pretty forever."

Where had she heard that? He had never said it aloud, he was certain, and never to her. Never to the girl who had been the culmination of the one dream he'd ever had, that he'd held through life and remembered through the fog of death, and the corrupt realisation of that dark dream come to haunt him. How had that thought, that dark compulsion that had been burnt away with the rest of his human drives, come to haunt him in the voice of the immortal beauty that had come to be his companion?

"I'm tired. When I wake up, we'll all be the same," said Emi.

She lay down, right there, in the dirt and the dancing light of what she'd done. With one hand beneath the sooty mass of her hair, she tucked one small fist up against her mouth, and he saw it. The carving. Long and narrow, only Christopher's bare feet and gaunt face stuck out from each end of Emi's hand. His story.

There seemed nothing to say. What use was there in arguing with a catastrophe? He might as well have asked an earthquake to be still, sung a tsunami to sleep. He stood and watched the little dead girl plummet into her impossible sleep, her lullaby the pop and crackle of burning wood and flesh.

He sat, legs crossed and hands on knees. He watched her, everything of the Old World either clutched in her hand or ended by it. If he sat there, quiet as can be, would she sleep forever?

No. She had always woken. And he could never tell when it would come.

He worked fast. From the destruction around him, he took the fire, careless of his singeing flesh, and oblivious when his dungarees caught aflame and fell away completely. He tore away what fell from him, and cast it aside. In the dying village's centre, he built the bonfire, a beacon at the centre of a smoke cloud that only thickened and thickened. In that cloud, when his work was done, when the great tongue of flame licked the night at his back, he found Emi. With care, he lifted her from the ashes, drawing her close to him. His large feet made clouds in the dirt as he returned and, with certain steps, climbed the kindling mount and into the wall of fire that he had made. There, with legs crossed, he laid his charge in his lap, cradling her head as the sooty bramble of her hair glowed gold once more and then was gone, as her dress fell away, and as the fire made a blackened mockery of her cherubim features. Soon, he could hold her no more, his arm giving way to the weight of her, and she splashed to ashes across the charred heaps of his knees. Thereafter, staring down into the place where she had been, the blackened trunk of Christopher fell also.

Thus ended what should have long, long ago.

Also available from the same author in print and eBook

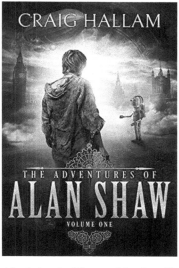

The Adventures of Alan Shaw is an epic Steampunk adventure spanning five incredible tales, from the author of Gothic Fantasy, Greaveburn.

For Alan Shaw, escaping the workhouse was only the beginning of the adventure. As an orphan growing up alone on the streets of Victorian London, staying alive is a daily battle, filled with choices a child should never have to make. This is Alan's lot in life, until he is offered more money than he can imagine; enough to take him to the new world to begin afresh. He only has to complete one task; something that could bring the British Empire to its knees.

In a series of adventures that take him from sea to sky, from Brighton to Bombay, Alan grows up in a steam-driven era where Automatons walk the streets of London and dirigibles master the air. Pitted against mad alchemists, tentacled submersibles, bomb-wielding saboteurs and the apocalyptic army of the Ordo Fenris, Alan has his work cut out for him. With a past as dark as his, who knows what Alan might grow up to be?

"Well written and entertaining."

"Written with considerable style"

"A considered dismantling of the macho hero archetype."